Robinson Public Library District
606 North Jefferson Street
Robinson, IL 62454-2699

The Long Journey

Another Vantage Press title by the author:

The Power of Love

The Long Journey

Persevere: Let Kindness
and Goodness Do the Rest

Marlowe "Red" Severson

VANTAGE PRESS
New York

Cover design by Susan Thomas

FIRST EDITION

All rights reserved, including the right of reproduction in whole or in part in any form.

Copyright © 2005 by Marlowe "Red" Severson

Published by Vantage Press, Inc.
419 Park Ave. South, New York, NY 10016

Manufactured in the United States of America
ISBN: 0-533-15137-6

Library of Congress Catalog Card No.: 2004195450

0 9 8 7 6 5 4 3 2 1

To all my basketball players, who did persevere

Contents

The Circumstance	1
A New Start	7
Botched Job	10
ADD	14
The Investigation	16
Pre-Depositions Trial	24
The Sentence	31
Prison	38
Time Passes	48
Parole and After	64
Ego/Mind Games	76
Back at Work	87
Ron Meets a Stranger	93
Truth and Knowledge Replace Perception	101
Journey's Reward	109

The Long Journey

The Circumstance

Elsie was a divorced mother whose only child, Ronnie, a sixteen-year-old, was living with her. Elsie was divorced two years ago from Glen, Ronnie's father. Glen was an abusive alcoholic. The couple had separated and reunited on three occasions but it didn't work out. Elsie had serious problems of her own. She was a very nervous individual who was subject to temper tantrums and unrestrained impatience, making it necessary for her to change residences more times than she wished to recall. She moved primarily because of her employment since she had more than ordinary difficulties with her fellow workers and her bosses.

Ronnie, the product of a dysfunctional family, had spent time in the world with parental problems. He argued with his mother frequently and wasn't too pleased about living with her. In fact, he had frequently contemplated leaving her and doing his thing. But then reality would set in and he sensed a small degree of security, so he remained unhappily in the home. Because of Ronnie's tendency to argue, Elsie wasn't sure she favored her son living with her, but what could she do? She had no other solution so the arrangement continued as it was.

An argument and physical confrontation occurred during one of their arguments and Ronnie pushed his mother away from him because she got into his face. Elsie threw a temper tantrum and picked up a fireplace iron. She struck him on the back of his right shoulder as he turned away to protect himself. Elsie had not intended to hurt him but only scare him. It did scare Ronnie and he fled from the house and never returned. He did what he had intended to do for some time. The next day, when his mother was at work, he returned home and packed his bag and left for good.

Even though Ronnie knew he must leave home, he also knew he loved his mom and would miss her. He recalled that they had shared some very joyful times since Glen, his father, and his mom divorced. But Ronnie told himself he must make a life for himself and would occasionally check in on his mother, but not until things "cooled."

A big problem was school. He was a sophomore at Lincoln High School. He questioned, how can I remain in school without any home or money? He decided he would drop out of school since he could not see another way and, besides, he had considered leaving school for a year but when he mentioned this to his mother, all hell broke out. Another huge argument resulted and Elsie would not hear of it. Now he was boss, school law would not force him to attend school since he was beyond the eighth grade and over sixteen years of age.

Ronnie had no close friends and only school acquaintances. He did very little socializing with anyone and it was said he had very few "buddies." School pupils did not attach to Ronnie because he was crude and rude and impolite; with a tendency to being a bully, he was overly aggressive. He often caused trouble and blamed the trouble on someone else. Other pupils got into trouble hanging with Ronnie. Ronnie had very little remorse about leaving school and few friends and "buddies" behind.

Ronnie was certainly in need of help and support. Where would he sleep, where would he eat? How would he obtain money? He sensed what it meant to be on his own. Mountainous obstacles were confronting a sixteen-year-old alone in a large city. Where to turn?

Many questions at once—and Ronnie didn't have his mom or a roof over his head; his life had always been constant and he had not worried about "minor" impediments to having a good time. Ronnie was totally confused, mixed up, and had great difficulty facing the situation. Just as he thought of something to do, he lost his attention and focus when another disturbing problem flashed into his mind. At this frustrating moment, he was reminded these were the same frustrating moments that had occurred in school and with daily tasks.

The lack of focus and concentration were haunting him. He realized it was, in his mind, more and more serious than it had been previous years in school and at home. He had no home, he had no money, and also, he had no teachers to counsel him. Ronnie was desperately alone and deserted. He thought about helplessness and hopelessness; but not quite so since he was strong and healthy. But how could he find work, any work? He noticed irritatingly that as one question came into his mind it was interrupted, replaced by another question and still others, a steady stream of questions and he admitted confusion reigned. How he missed his mom and his teachers! But reconciliation was not possible. He had cut the ties and must stick with his new freedom.

Ronnie passed a large food supply warehouse and an adjoining supermarket. In the window he noticed a "help needed" sign. He didn't hesitate to enter the supermarket and asked for the person in charge. He was told Bill was the general manager. Ronnie was escorted into Bill's office and was very apprehensive, more so than if he were meeting a girlfriend's father for the first time. He told Bill

he noticed the "help wanted sign" in the store window and had come to apply for the job.
 Bill sized him up and said, "You look strong and we need strong young bodies to lift boxes. Some boxes weigh as much as one hundred pounds. Can you do that?"
 Ronnie quickly replied, "Yes."
 Ronnie was told that the available work was a part-time job of four hours a day. Could he handle four hours of heavy lifting each day? Of course he could. His very first job!
 Bill, the manager, explained that the job was a 1:00 A.M. until 5:00 A.M. job, Wednesday through Saturday. He would assist the shelf stockers by bringing boxes of supplies up front on a buoy cart, load the boxes on the cart and then rush the cart into the store for the stockers.
 Ronnie was not taken back by the working hours. He did not care, it was a job and it beat starving. He would work twenty hours a week at a minimum wage of five dollars an hour. Ronnie had no problem figuring his daily income and determined he'd earn twenty dollars per day. That was a lot of money for a sixteen-year-old and he was very content to know he'd earn food money and room money. It was a very promising start and he was proud of himself.
 Bill decided he'd take a chance on Ronnie and give him the job. Ronnie quickly accepted and was told to report that next morning at 1:00 A.M. Before leaving, he filled out all the necessary payroll forms and the formal application form. He left the address line blank since he had not acquired a room as yet, but that would be his very next move. He did not locate a room right away and thought of returning to Bill's office and ask him if he could bunk in the warehouse until he could find a place. But Bill did not know Ronnie and surely might wonder if

he was a runaway or someone in trouble with the police. Ronnie couldn't do that and place his newfound job in jeopardy. What next?

He had not resolved his sleeping problem yet. But he must do that immediately, as he was shivering at the thought of the homeless, bums, and tramps living on the streets and sleeping in the gutter wells along the buildings. He shivered more from fear and resolved being a bum was not the solution.

It was 6:00 P.M. and he would stay around the supermarket and keep on the move until it came time to report for his first night of work. Before it was too late, he'd enjoy an evening meal of a single burger, small fries, and a small shake. He noticed a special at $1.89 and burning pocket money of $2.00 could cover it. He finished the meal and still felt hungry, a poor situation heading to work, but it would have to do. His mind was hot; it felt afire and racing fast. Ron had ascertained he would complement his supper with fresh fruit and milk from the super market. He'd do this while at work and knew he could find plenty of opportunity to do so.

He made it through his first day at work and four hours went very fast. Don was his first working partner. Don was a friendly guy, too friendly, and asked too many questions. Ron resented this and felt it was not Don's business to question his background. Don got the message and they worked through the remainder of the shift with little conversation.

Ronnie was able to handle the workload. In fact Bill, his boss, noticed the new man was a find. The manager told him he was doing fine. This pleased Ronnie. But a personality problem arose—he could not tolerate Don, his working partner. Three weeks later, Ronnie noticed Don wasn't working his shift with him. He wondered if Don had quit. Then, a week after that, after working alone on the shift, Ron confronted Don when he saw him on another crew. He asked about his absence from their shift and Don told him he requested a shift change and had been reassigned. Short fused, this angered Ronnie and he told Don he didn't like working with him either. Offended, Don told Ron he was a flake. Ron knew what a flake was and a fight ensued. It was a fierce struggle until finally their fellow workers separated them. They went back to their respective posts and Ron was cussing under his breath and still very angry. He'd show Don later on when given a chance. But, for now, it was over and Ron felt nothing more would be said. But he was wrong, very wrong.

He existed in this manner for two years. Ron would find another job but then his erratic temperament and strange behavior would cost him the job. He was very confused, angry, and always blaming co-employees or bosses—or both. So disturbed, he decided enough is enough. I'll see what's for me in the big time and he knew he would need some new contacts to accomplish this. It kept resurfacing and haunting him—he had no day-to-day contact with his mom, he had no contact with any teacher or counselor, and there were no school acquaintances to harass. He was very lonesome, many questions flashing through his mind, and characteristically very unpredictable. And as he lost each job, his temperament and unpredictability worsened. He concluded that he would never take another job and struggle through this anymore, never again.

A New Start

During two plus years in the city working sporadically on several jobs, all in the same vicinity, he'd come upon four guys who appeared to be his age and were buddies because they were always together and seemingly enjoying one another's company. They regularly were shooting craps or playing twenty-one and occasionally poker. Until his current appearance, he'd never asked or been told what each of the group did for work. He certainly wondered since they were all dressed well and each owned a car. They had become accustomed to him and liked him. Jud, a mouthpiece for the others, asked Ron if he would like to earn real money and fast.

Ron's thinking was way off on this one and wondered what Jud was speaking about and so he asked, "What kind of work is it?" Jud replied, "We have a lucrative, bullet-proof profession."

Ron quickly asked, "What profession is it?" He was completely naïve and in the dark about all this. He knew Ron would certainly be interested in some cash since he'd been operating with little money.

Jud pulled no punches and said, "Burglary. We knock off exclusive vacant homes when the owners are away. The homes are well cased and, after satisfactory surveillance, we determine when it is safe."

Ron looked at Jud and said, "I have never done anything like this."

Jud replied, "Ron, you need no experience, we'll train

you." Jud continued, "Ron, this is how we earn our nice cars, nice clothes, and our drugs."

Ronnie was vulnerable at this point in his life due to all the unprecedented events happening to him, but he was observant and certainly he did know about marijuana though he wasn't sure about other drugs. But to think no heavier drugs were used was utterly naïve—and that he was not.

Lou, another of the group, said, "Some of us double up Juana and Coke." All wanted to smoke some Juana and a little later do a snort or two. Lou snorted some Coke and showed Ronnie how to do it.

Ron became a member of the group, now five in all, and was learning the drug ropes while waiting to participate in a full-scale big-time burglary. To this point, Ron had participated in a few small petty entry-and-run jobs but all the while enjoying Juana and occasionally some Coke. He was beginning to become comfortable with life and thought *what a life! Where have I been all this time?* He was enjoying a life of leisure on easy street with no regular work schedule to meet.

The gang knew whose homes they burglarized. The job they were currently planning belonged to a wealthy single man who commuted weekly to Chicago. Through the close surveillance they learned that, the businessman was away from the home Monday through Wednesday. So anytime from Monday through Wednesday, they could do the job. The group had not robbed this specific home but they were certain other similar operatives had visited it. They made final plans and gave assignments to each group each member, to be carried out like clockwork: a driver, the cover men, one equipment man (e.g. crowbar etc.), two entry men and looters, and one entry man, a gunman, to protect the two entry men. Ronnie was the gunman. Each member carried a gun but only for individual protection. If there was any unsuspected interruption or intrusion, Ronnie's job was to insure the operation was successful.

Botched Job

They entered the residence and immediately began to loot the premises and, an instant later, were interrupted when a voice shouted, "Hands up, you're covered! Move and I'll shoot to kill."

The man behind the commanding voice snapped on a light and appeared with an imposing gun. He had the gun aimed at the two looters. Ronnie nervously saw what was happening and, in his usually easily aroused state and his mind afire, delivered rapid gun-like thoughts into his brain. This state made him panic without any chance to review the situation and he fired three shots into the surprised guard who had not seen him step from his hiding place. The guard went to the floor fatally wounded and all of the gang members inside the house departed quickly toward the escape car and they sped away.

What happened? What happened? shouted all members simultaneously.

Phil answered, "There was a guard hiding inside the house, he jumped us and ordered us to put our hands up since he had a gun and would shoot to kill, then Ron bolted from his hiding place and fired three shots into the guard. Ron fired without requesting the guard to drop his gun because he was covered."

Jud was furious and angrily asked, "Ron, why did you act so impulsively? Why couldn't the three of you disarm the guard, why couldn't you order the guard to drop his gun since you had the drop on him? Now we'll be sought as murderers!" he uttered as he turned away from Ron.

He whirled around to face all of them. He was stone-faced white as if seeing a ghost but angrier with Ron. Then uttered dejectedly, "We'll be sought for murder but remember, Ron shot the man."

Ron was flabbergasted. He did not expect Jud to be so cowardly and running down Ronnie's spine were chills he'd never ever experienced before, and now he was a murderer—*help me someone!*

The burglary was headline news and, all media reported, rightly so. It was their lead news story. The burglars wondered what clues they might have left and concluded there were fingerprints galore since the unexpected interruption by the house guard had left them without time to wipe the place clean. And there would be bullet casings as well as escape car tire prints.

Jud knew they "blew it" and he stated it would be only a matter of a several days before they were implicated. Yes, they were as good as caught but what should they do? It was not easy to flee the city with so many clues left behind. Where could they hide out?

It appeared a hopeless situation for the gang. In two days they were arrested and arraigned separately and the experienced detectives knew how to get to a killer or killers in a gang. The police were masters in getting suspects to crack and to confess. Quickly all members began to "snitch and rat" on the others in order to save their own hides. Headed by Jud, the gang members pointed the finger at Ron and said he was the one who pulled the trigger; Ron did the shooting.

Court

The county and state attorney brought burglary and murder charges. The usual arraignment was made in court and all gang members were arraigned on armed robbery and murder. The four, other than Ron, were charged as accomplices to the charges but Ron was charged with first-degree capital murder along with armed robbery. He had pulled the trigger, shot the guard, and had been fingered by his fellow gang members. First-degree capital murder can call for the death penalty. *What am I to do?* Ron, utterly shocked, frightened, and subdued in more ways than one.

Someone told Ron he was in dire need of an attorney. He readily agreed but without any financial resources, Ron was assigned a Public Attorney, Terrill, an experienced public defender who was known as a good, thorough attorney.

The first thing Terrill did was have an extensive and exhaustive interview with his client, now charged with capital murder. He then reviewed the interview data and observed, during the interview, that Ron was indecisive, repeating over and over as if he had forgotten the question, unsure of things and certainly unsure of himself, unable to focus for any length of time on Attorney Terrill's questions.

Terrill said that Ron's behavior was not normal and he would check this matter further. Perhaps this could lead to something beneficial to defense plans. But on some concise information he had learned from Ron's interview, Ron told him of his father's alcohol addiction and abuse. Ron also stated that his mother, Elsie, had a terrible temper and lacked focus and consistency. Coupled with this information and Terrill's first-hand observations of Ron, Attorney Terrill thought to himself *this is a very dysfunctional family of the first order.* Attorney Terrill had experience with and some knowledge of ADD, Attention Deficit Disorder, and he also decided he'd petition the court for an ADD evaluation of Ron. It would have to be allowed and done for Ron's protection and defense.

ADD

ADD, Terrill knew, was hereditary and he also knew that if a mother suffered ADD, a high percentage of the time so will her son. This common knowledge resulted from research about ADD. Terrill had also read that ADD is a chronic disorder which affects five to eight percent of young people, children included. Attention Deficit Disorder manifests in early childhood and commonly persists throughout adulthood. The attorney was aware the condition creates frustration and disappointments at home, school, and on the job. Finally, Terrill reminded himself that his department had come in contact with ADD prisoners who demonstrated through their diagnosis they'd had the crippling condition from childhood. He was highly suspicious that Ron might be one of ADD's latest victims, his condition caused by a dysfunctional family since he'd learned from Ron that his dad was an abusive alcoholic and his mother possibly suffering ADD. He aimed to find out.

In the first court appearance, Terrill asked the judge to order an Attention Deficit Disorder evaluation. He informed the judge of Ron's family situation and explained the details that Ron provided. Attorney Terrill told the judge he had first-hand observed these ADD characteristics: short attention span, distractibility, procrastination, disorganization, impulsiveness, and hyperactivity. Terrill and the judge felt it extremely important and essential for Ron to be thoroughly evaluated and diagnosed. And if diagnosed with ADD, the attorney would build his life-saving defense case around this fact. Ron, Terrill felt strongly, was suffering from ADD. The judge didn't hesitate to grant and issue an ADD evaluation/diagnosis for Ron.

After twenty hours of intensive evaluation by a highly trained diagnostic specialist in the ADD disorder field, the conclusive result from the evaluation was that Ron suffered from acute ADD. Furthermore, the specialist seemed to agree with Terrill's suggestion that perhaps Ron's mother was suffering from the disorder too.

The immediate question in the Attorney's mind, the ADD specialist's mind, and the Court Judge's mind was how did Ron's condition endure throughout his first eighteen years? Weren't the parents aware, the teachers, the school counselors aware? Wasn't someone aware and wanting to help Ron? The answer to all these questions was yes, but in many such cases the symptoms categorize the victim as a dull, naughty, troublemaker and outright dumb. Most certainly everyone in contact with Ron—and certainly his parents, school officials, and employers—could have and should have heard Ron's call for help.

The Investigation

Ron was arraigned for armed robbery and first-degree murder. The public defender, Terrill, had acquired information about the history, of Ron Wilson's childhood and early adulthood. Judge Lowell had granted an ADD (Attention Deficit Disorder) evaluation. The evaluation and resulting diagnosis indicated Ron as suffering acute ADD.

Attorney Terrill was certain he would find information and evidence Ron was living in a very dysfunctional family and a family of alcoholism, abuse, and divorce. Glen, Ron's father, was an alcoholic who had physically abused Ron and his mother, Elsie. Both mother and son were physically and emotionally abused. Elsie was very hyper. She had abused Ron emotionally and attempted to abuse him physically with a fireplace poker iron. Ron told Attorney Terrill that his mother had experienced more than one anxiety episode. She had, on occasion, pounded the walls and pulled at her hair. Elsie had left Glen twice and then she reunited with him but it didn't change a thing. Ron told Terrill that Elsie finally divorced Glen and, Ron stated, the time following the divorce was a peaceful time for him since he didn't have to choose sides.

Terrill began investigating the information Ron had given him. He needed substantial evidence to support alcoholism and abuse, as the court would not accept hearsay. Where would he begin? He decided to begin with Ron's home and his mother, Elsie.

Lincoln School, Ron's teachers and counselors, would

be his next visit. While at the school he would visit Ron's classmates. Ron's employment record was brief because of his age. He had worked at part-time jobs. But any employer could provide needed background information. A final visit would be with the police department.

Ron gave Terrill his mom's address and her telephone number. Attorney Terrill attempted to call Elsie but learned that her telephone was disconnected. He decided to visit Elsie. He went to the address and learned Elsie no longer lived there. Where was she? He must locate her; so he visited the post office. Upon identifying himself, he was provided a forwarding address. Terrill went directly to the forwarding address.

Late in the afternoon, Terrill rang the doorbell; he waited. Several rings later, a frail woman of small stature answered the door.

Attorney Terrill asked, "Are you Elsie?"

She was hesitant and appeared frightened. The attorney observed her hesitation and confusion and said, "I am a friend of Ron's. May I visit with you?"

Elsie relaxed and became interested. "Yes, I am Elsie. Where is Ron? Is he okay? Has something happened to him?"

Terrill observed she had been incommunicado. Elsie had changed addresses, she was not working, and obviously had not read the newspapers. She had no contact with Ron.

Again, Terrill said he was Ron's attorney and asked, "May I come in?"

Elsie opened the door and showed him into her living room. He began to bring her up to date with Ron's situation. Elsie didn't seem shocked about the news. Had she been expecting the worst? Unexpectedly she became aroused, anxious, and clutched Attorney Terrill's suit coat lapel. The attorney was surprised as he witnessed a change of demeanor and an aggressive nature. Elsie asked, "Where is he? Can I see him, are they harming Ron?" She loved her son and she wanted to be with him. She displayed unmistaken motherly love. Just as quickly as Elsie reacted, she backed away from Terrill and slumped into her chair.

Elsie spoke to attorney Terrill, " I will do anything to help my son, I will do anything you ask of me."

Ron's attorney informed Elsie of the serious charges filed against Ron and explained that Ron would need her support in his defense.

Attorney Terrill spoke, "Ron faces a very stiff sentence which calls for life in prison." He informed Elsie he would need information to verify Ron's story. Elsie urgently said she would oblige.

"What did Ron say?" she quizzed. Then the attorney provided the detail Ron had offered him.

Elsie verified Ron's story. Terrill was very pleased to learn Ron had not lied. Attorney Terrill would not question Ron's truthfulness and he was grateful he had not been misled.

Elsie became anxious once again and seemed obsessed with the idea Ron was in jail. The attorney solaced her by saying he would do everything within his means to help Ron through his predicament. He thanked Elsie for her honesty.

As he left he said, "I will be in contact with you and inform you of the proceedings. Elsie, you will be very critical to Ron's defense."

He gave her his card and permission to contact him at any time and he asked Elsie to keep him informed of her whereabouts.

Elsie said she could and would expect to hear from him soon.

As Attorney Terrill walked down the steps away from Elsie, he assured himself of his gratefulness for Ron's truthfulness but he also noted, Ron is a victim of a dysfunctional home. This fact would be the basis of Ron's defense case. Where would he go next to gather witnesses to support the facts he had? He reached for the address of Lincoln High School and got into his car.

The principal of Lincoln High School said it did not surprise her Ron Wilson was in a dire situation. Attorney Terrill did not ask a question but the principal began discussing Ron in seriousness. She was eager to talk about Ron and began to discuss his family. Also, she seemed amazed that Ron had remained in school. She had expected him to drop out of school.

As the principal explained to Terrill, Ron had a good attendance record and was no truant. She mentioned Ron's grades were not good because he had great difficulty concentrating and focusing. He was motivated to learn but couldn't maintain his concentration. Initially, he was interested, but then his interest deserted him before he could complete a challenge. Ron's attention span was very short and he was a notorious underachiever. Why Ron had not received counseling to help him she did not know. Attorney Terrill had intended to inquire about counseling but the principal had already given her answer; she didn't know. Apparently little interest in Ron at Lincoln High was the fact.

The attorney asked the principal how Ron was accepted and treated by his classmates, peers. She said Ron regularly was in trouble with other students, not occasionally but often. The principal noted that Ron had a short fuse and a nasty temper. Other students had little to do with Ron for this reason. He was a troublemaker and the students did not want his reputation to come down on them. Ron would get other students in trouble and often did, she said. Then suddenly the principal shifted gears and told Mr. Terrill Ron could be a very good student and a nice person if given a chance. (A chance by whom? And why wasn't he given a chance?) Attorney Terrill asked himself why not and why no encouragement from Lincoln High officials/teachers? It puzzled Terrill and he searched for answers. Here's a youngster apparently of good intelligence and potential but doesn't receive help or encouragement to excel. Attorney Terrill dismissed himself with a thank you and said good day.

Jim, a close friend and one of few Ron had at school, sat down and faced Mr. Terrill. Jim appeared timid and lacking in confidence. He was lost without a leader, he was truly a follower. The attorney said hello and quickly told Jim why he was there. "Jim, I must ask you about Ron Wilson, your friend. Jim, Ron is in serious trouble, legal trouble."

Jim did not seem surprised and said, "I knew it." Terrill asked Jim, "What do you mean, you knew it?"

Jim did not pause and said, "Ron was always looking for fights and he was a bully, he would pick on and abuse others, especially those smaller and weaker than he. Ron would gain a friend and a short time later he would quarrel and fight with his new friend and this happened over and over."

Attorney Terrill now heard first-hand of Ron's bad behavior among his classmates. Ron was exhibiting and suffering from ADD. Terrill was certain Ron had to be in control and in his social life and it caused turmoil for him. ADD is like a blanket hiding positive behavioral characteristics. The attorney didn't need to ask; he knew why

Jim remained "tight" with Ron. He was afraid of Ron. Ron made Jim his social slave.

It was time to call it a day. Any other interviews must wait but he recognized it was a good day. Attorney Terrill felt more positive about Ron's situation and he was thankful Ron was honest with him and knew he could trust Ron. Even after several interviews with several negative characterizations, the attorney sensed goodness in his client. Terrill liked Ron Wilson. But he would be careful about over-attachment with his client. The attorney told himself, *I have some difficult decisions ahead and cannot permit personal feelings to influence my decisions.* He would work diligently with commitment to Ron.

Attorney Terrill arose early at 7:00 A.M. and was on his way to police headquarters by 9:00 A.M. He entered the station and introduced himself to the desk sergeant. Terrill asked for the policeman who covered Elsie Wilson's neighborhood. The officer was Patrolman Stevens. Patrolman Stevens shook hands with attorney Terrill. The attorney inquired about Elsie Wilson's neighborhood. He was told it was a typical, peaceful residential area. The neighborhood had its occasional burglary and from time to time a stolen vehicle. And it had some domestic problems. Patrolman Stevens told the attorney he had been dispatched to Elsie Wilson's home more than once to prevent a drunken Glen Wilson from abusing Elsie and on occasion Ron, his son.

The policeman asserted Glen Wilson was an alcoholic and, when drunk, abusive. Officer Stevens reported Elsie had evicted Glen from the home and had filed a restraining order. In time, Glen would return home and it started over again. Patrolman Stevens said Elsie could stand it no more and she divorced Glen. Attorney Terrill asked if Ron had been arrested and was told he had not been. Ron had a clean record. Terrill was relieved and knew Ron with no previous record would be in good standing with the court. The attorney thanked the police officer and felt Patrolman Stevens would be a strong witness in Ron's trial.

St. John's Parish was on Cleveland Street and Terrill knew it would be just off Washburn Avenue. He turned off Washburn Avenue and parked in the St. John's church lot. He headed to the parish center where he was met by Reverend Joseph.

As Reverend Joseph informed Attorney Terrill, Ron had attended pre-confirmation instruction but his mother moved and they left the parish. The reverend doubted Ron had been confirmed but he told the attorney Ron had been an observant, questioning student.

Ron asked about the crucifixion of Christ. He was questioning the fact since he couldn't believe God would punish his Son, Jesus Christ, to save us from sin and death. Reverend Joseph said Ron wanted to learn about the crucifixion and our redemption. The reverend concluded, "I believe Ron is a good prospect for Christ. It would be a surprise if he doesn't turn out successful." Attorney Terrill was heartened by the minister's remarks portraying Ron as a willing spiritual student. Reverend Joseph would be a good character witness.

The attorney had momentum and, after each interview, he felt more assured for Ron's chances. Ron had been fairly characterized and seemed to be a typical young man who wasn't beyond youthful mischief, but was also a curious young man who was interested in improving his awareness and consciousness. Mr. Terrill was becoming aware that Ron Wilson had become and is a victim of his environment. A point he must prove to the court.

He reached for his note pad in his suit coat. H_ interviewed everyone on his list? No, he had one impo_ tant contact he must make. He must talk with Bill, the supermarket manager, Ron's boss.

Bill was a large man who was friendly and curious to learn about Ron. Bill remembered Ron well and said simply, "He was one of my very best hires." Bill described Ron as strong, willing, and punctual. He did not miss work. Bill said Ron worked for him for five months and strangely disappeared.

Bill asked, "Is Ron in trouble? Where is he?"

Attorney Terrill explained Ron's problem and his incarceration. Terrill asked if Bill would be a witness for Ron. Bill advised the attorney that he would.

Ron's fellow gang members would not be interviewed at this time. The attorney would wait until he had a subpoena served on each member. He did not want to visit with them until he had them on the witness stand; but he certainly was interested in talking with Jud, the gang leader and mouthpiece. Jud had reminded other members of the gang that Ron was the killer and don't forget it.

Pre-Depositions Trial

Much happened in the month following the botched burglary. It was time for the pre-trial hearings. The prosecutor and the defense attorney submitted a list of witnesses and took depositions. The depositions when completed are presented to the court and the prosecution and defense receive the depositions for their examination preparing for the trial. The date was the 10th of June. The trial was scheduled to begin sometime in the second week of July. The trial would be in District Court in Hennepin County, State of Minnesota. There had been no request for a change of venue.

The presiding judge selected was Judge Lowell. Attorney Terrill was pleased as he knew Judge Lowell to be fair. Judge Lowell was referred to as the "forgiving judge," a respected second chance believer if circumstances permitted a second chance. Judge Lowell appealed to all fairness and would facilitate an environment for a possible second chance. The judge was also an advocate for the young and he supported rehabilitation so the young could right themselves and become respectable citizens.

The prosecutor, Mitchell, knew the judge was meticulous and would search the evidence seeking an opportunity for the court to support every defendant's possibility. Mitchell was confident the prosecution had a guilty verdict in hand but was concerned about the penalty phase. The prosecutor would strive for a jury trial and provide some influence on the penalty phase. He did not cherish

Judge Lowell determining the penalty. Defense Attorney Terrill would oppose a jury trial and would prompt a plea bargain for Ron. The penalty would be assessed by the judge. This was conjecture and pre-trial maneuvering.

The trial began on July 13. Judge Lowell addressed the jury briefly and final instructions would be given later. He introduced the jury to the prosecutor and defense attorneys. The judge requested that Mr. Mitchell, the prosecutor, speak first. The prosecutor reviewed the prosecution's charges against Ron Wilson and said the facts will prove Ron Wilson is guilty of burglary and murder and he, Ron Wilson, must be found guilty.

Mr. Mitchell sat down.

Defense Attorney Terrill then spoke as Ron Wilson's attorney. He stated Ron Wilson was not guilty and that the defense would present evidence to prove Mr. Wilson's innocence. "We believe you must return a not guilty verdict." The legal battle is set, a battle to determine Ron Wilson's future.

Defense attorney Terrill reviewed in his mind his defensive scheme. Ron Wilson was suffering from ADD (Attention Deficit Disorder) and specifically ADOD (Attention Deficit of Obsessive Disorder). He would support this with documentation and evaluation diagnostic procedures. The attorney would employ medical witnesses and mind, personality specialists, e.g., psychologists and psychiatrists. Other witnesses such as teachers, friends, employers, and police would present Ron as he is. He would like to employ Elsie Wilson, Ron's mother, but at this time he wasn't sure he would or should call her to the witness stand. This was the defensive framework, scheme, the plan to save Ron from life imprisonment without parole. Terrill's plan did not call for a non-guilty verdict since established fact pointed to Ron as the killer of the home guard.

A very good attorney begins from the end and proceeds from the beginning to achieve the ending. Attorney Terrill saw the ending and was proceeding to plan for the beginning. If the defense could establish ADD as the culprit and establish Ron's characteristics to be ADD characteristics so the jury would agree that Ron was suffering from the terrible, debilitating illness ADD, then Ron would be subject to a favorable ending. The jury must see Ron had no control of himself when ADD had its grip on him. The attorney could expect the medical witnesses to point out the difference between Ron's illness and a disease; he suffered from an illness for which there is no one cause and very difficult to treat—but a true disease is caused by a germ or a virus, and can be treated with antibiotics. So far, Ron Wilson suffered from a very tragic, debilitating illness—but not from a disease.

Ron's defense attorney, Terrill, would repeat over and over that Ron was a victim of a potential killer, ADD. Terrill ended his imaginary defense scenario and began to concentrate on bombarding the judge and jury with the unpredictable and destructive traits of ADD that Ron had no control over.

The defense decided against a temporary insanity plea even though Ron might have lost contact with right or wrong and was temporarily insane. He, Terrill, ruled against an insanity plea because he foresaw the medical witnesses examining that possibility. He need not.

The prosecutor reviewed his case in confidence of a "guilty" verdict. Facts had revealed Ron Wilson was the gunman. Terrill must concentrate on the penalty phase. For now, Attorney Mitchell knew that first-degree murder and death was not a viable verdict. He would, in due time, move that the desired penalty be murder and life imprisonment.

Attorney Mitchell felt that in all probability a jury would accept the defense's argument that Ron was and is a victim. Ron's age, 20 years, was in his favor to receive some consideration from the jurors. He was young, strong, and clean appearing. Yes, Mitchell's best approach would be to obtain a guilty statement from Ron Wilson with agreement that the State of Minnesota would accept life imprisonment. And he was convinced life imprisonment would "fly" with defense attorney Terrill.

It appeared the defense held some "big cards" and Terrill was shrewd and sharp and expected to play them with a plea arrangement, perhaps even a parole. If the prosecuting attorney, Mitchell, believed the defense had a favorable jury along with a sympathetic judge, he might be compelled to bargain a certain length of imprisonment and parole after 25 years. Mitchell tossed his head back, looked skyward and resolved we'll have a guilty verdict and then the jury/judge will pronounce the justice, sentence.

July 13 the trial began. Judge Lowell presiding and both attorneys ready. The jury had been seated in the jury box. In the same instant, Judge Lowell instructed the police to bring Ron Wilson into the courtroom. The bailiff was instructed to seat Ron at the defense table next to Terrill.

Court began with Judge Lowell introducing the court to the jury. "In District Court in Hennepin County, Minneapolis, Minnesota on this day, July 13, the State charges Ron Wilson with murder. Representing the State of Minnesota is Attorney Mitchell, the prosecutor and representing the defendant, Ron Wilson, is Attorney Terrill."

Then Judge Lowell said, "Mr. Mitchell, you may proceed."

The prosecutor began. "Your Honor, members of the jury. We, the State of Minnesota, will prove that Ron Wilson," and he pointed to Ron Wilson at the defense table, "willfully shot three times Mr. Stanley Simons thereby causing his instantaneous death. It was a needless, vicious act in which Mr. Simons was ambushed without warning. He had no opportunity to protect himself. We will prove that Ron Wilson, the defendant, in the presence of three others, was the killer as attested to by his gang members. Also, the defendant testified to the police that he did the shooting. With the defendant's admission, and the testimony of scene witnesses, we will prove his guilt and ask the jury and court to find Ron Wilson, sitting over there," (and he pointed at Ron), "guilty of first-degree murder." Prosecutor Mitchell sat down at the prosecutor's table.

Judge Lowell said, "Mr. Terrill, you may proceed."

Defense Attorney Terrill rose and replied, "Your Honor, members of the jury. We will prove without a doubt that Ron Wilson is a tragic victim of a serious illness, an illness with no single cause, but an illness with several causes, a disease which shows no mercy to its victim. Ron Wilson is a victim of ADD (Attention Deficit Disorder). Ron Wilson is a classic victim; he is no more than an adolescent, a mere child. ADD's victims can include anyone: child, woman, and man—young and old alike. ADD has no preferences. Medical witnesses, doctors, and specialists will present clear, concise, factual information portraying the destructive nature of ADD. Your Honor, members of this jury, my client, Ron Wilson, has not confessed to murder and we plead not guilty; furthermore, we will prove Ron Wilson not guilty."

The prosecution was first to summon its witnesses. After each witness had been cross-examined by the defense, the witnesses were cross-examined by the prosecutor, Mitchell. During the third day of witnesses' interviews and cross-examination, as the trial was moving rapidly and smoothly, Judge Lowell called for an hour recess, a longer recess than usual, and the two attorneys were summoned into the Judge's chamber.

Following the meeting in Judge Lowell's chambers with both attorneys, it seemed clear a break-through in trial proceedings had occurred. Attorney Mitchell, the prosecutor, had observed the jury was reacting favorably to the defense witnesses. He also observed an enthusiastic response by Judge Lowell regarding the defense witnesses' testimony. Mr. Mitchell was experienced in courtroom antics and because of this, he would visit with attorney Terrill to assess where he might be headed.

Mr. Mitchell, the prosecutor, felt a life term for Ron Wilson might be in jeopardy and he had best act to insure an acceptable verdict. Attorney Terrill sensed the momentum on Ron's side and knew this momentum could swing at any time. He knew he had an edge. Apply it. Terrill, too, was experienced and he too knew a sure thing for Ron would be to cut a deal with the prosecution. If Terrill would cut a deal, it must be for 25 years with parole at the end of 12-1/2 years, no less.

The two attorneys began to negotiate. The prosecutor offered a life term with no parole. Terrill said, "No deal!" He stated, "We will agree to a twenty-five-year term with parole after 12-1/2 years." Terrill's persistence prevailed and Mitchell felt he held the "trump card." Prosecutor

Mitchell agreed to accept Ron Wilson's plea for a sentence of 25 years and parole after 12-1/2 years.

The attorneys approached Judge Lowell's bench and announced a plea bargain. Ron Wilson would be sentenced to 25 years with parole after 12-1/2 years. The Judge looked at the attorneys and told them to write up a brief with all details. Both must sign it and return it to him in the morning before court convenes. If Judge Lowell accepted the plea agreement, things were going well for Ron Wilson. Mr. Terrill would inform his client things were going well for him. After Judge Lowell's examination of all details and acceptance of the plea agreement the judge would address the jury, announce the court's acceptance, and declare the trial over.

The judge would determine sentence and would also assess the penalty. Would the judge impose a sentence that would include Ron's treatment of ADD? And perhaps, more positively, would Judge Lowell provide a provision for Ron's high school education?

Tomorrow these questions would be answered.

The Sentence

With pre-sentence hearings completed, it was time for the sentencing. Judge Lowell had Ron Wilson brought to the courthouse. He entered the courtroom handcuffed wearing a dark blue sport coat and light gray slacks. Ron looked at his mother and smiled and reading lips said, "I love you, I'm alright." She was in tears and barely controlling herself.

The bailiff seated Ron at the defense table next to his attorney, Terrill.

Judge Lowell spoke, "Will the defendant rise?"

The attorney nudged Ron to stand and face Judge Lowell.

Judge Lowell said, "The State of Minnesota, represented by prosecutor, Mr. Mitchell, and defendant, Mr. Wilson, represented by Mr. Terrill have entered into a plea agreement. I, Judge Lowell, representing the District Court of Minnesota have agreed to accept the plea agreement."

Judge Lowell looked at Ron Wilson, "How do you plead?" Ron Wilson answered, "Your Honor, I plead guilty" in a clear, strong and sincere voice.

Judge Lowell asked Ron, "Do you wish to make a statement?"

Ron replied, "Yes, Your Honor. I am sorry for my deed and ask forgiveness since I know of no other way to express the feelings deep inside my heart, feelings which constantly remind me of my shame, guilt, and remorse."

Ron looked into Judge Lowell's eyes and said, "Your

Honor, I am sorry and I accept my punishment." Ron was excused to take his seat at the defense table.

The judge said, "What I am about to say will take some time."

The judge began. "The defendant, Ron Wilson, has pleaded guilty to first-degree murder and has plea bargained, agreeing to a prison term of 25 years with parole after 12-1/2 years. The court has accepted the plea bargain. However, before this court releases the defendant to the prison authorities, several court stipulations will be required and must be fulfilled on behalf of Ron Wilson and the court will implement follow-up procedures periodically to assure the court's mandates are fulfilled.

"This court approved a pre-trial neuropsychological evaluation. The evaluation determined that Ron Wilson suffers from ADD and ADOD and acutely. ADD is Attention Deficit Disorder and the O refers to Obsessive, without control. Ron Wilson was subjected to the very best, newest, evaluative techniques. The defendant was interviewed about home, school, employment and social experiences. Other tests administered indicated his state of being were intelligence, academic skills, problem solving (verbal and non verbal), abstract reasoning, cognitive flexibility, organizational skills, planning, attention-concentration, memory, language skills, visual special abilities, and emotional-personality functioning. These tests indicated a degree of Ron Wilson's disability.

"Also, scientific tests were employed. The biofeedback study has been helpful in reducing the amount of drugs the ADD victim takes. The specific test of the biofeedback group was neurofeedback, a monitoring test that measures electrical activity in the brain. Emotion produces electrical energy that is found in the brain's center. The brain centers have specific responsibilities to perform. Negative emotions surface in the right side of the brain and positive emotions are created in the left side of the brain. Biofeedback techniques produce a change, adjustment of the activities of the brain centers. In treatment, the clinician can reduce the activity in the right brain, he/she uses a very specific biofeedback program and the same is so for the left brain. The clinician will employ a very specific biofeedback program to train the left brain chamber.

"In a brochure located by my research aide, I learned of a study that excited me and I want to share it with you. The study conducted by Dr. Joel Lubar, originated at the University of Tennessee, indicated that neurofeedback could reduce symptoms of Attention Deficit Disorder (ADD). The study indicates the patients pay greater attention and have an average boost in IQ of up to 20 points after 20–60 sessions."

The judge continued. "A second scientific test administered to Ron Wilson was the quantitative electroencophology (EEG and qEEG). The test measures the electrical activity in the cerebral cortex of the brain. The results of the test help diagnoses mental health conditions, through statistical evaluation of the electrical activity of the cortex. The reliability of this scientific test is equal to and greater than the more common MRI (Magnetic Resonance Imagery) and the CAT scan (Computerized Axial Tomography).

"The EEG test shows there are brain waves of various frequencies, some fast and some slow. These frequency bands are: Delta, Theta, Alpha, and Beta. ADD victims tend to have slow waves (usually Delta, slow Theta, and sometimes excessive low frequency Alpha). When excessive slow wave activity is present in the frontal part of the cerebral cortex, individuals can experience difficulty controlling attention and their emotions. These persons may have serious problems with concentration, memory, mood shifts, impulse control, and may often experience hyperactivity. Added to this scenario, persons may exhibit lowered intellectual efficiency. Many outside observers unfamiliar with ADD often times characterized ADD victims as dull, bullying, mean, and dumb."

The judge stopped to sip some water and catch his breath. It was clear to all the courtroom that the judge was very interested in Ron Wilson's condition, ADD.

The judge spoke again. "The court's aides, as directed, located two ADD victims who agreed to an interview with the court. Each interviewee impressed upon the court that drugs were not the solution. Drugs do nothing to alleviate causes of ADD. Like most drugs, the body will acclimate to the drug and then go on to the next drug. And so it goes as the body adjusts to a drug, and then you are back to square one while the illness progresses. Causes are not eliminated just veiled. Drugs work on the symptoms and, only for a time, not on the causes. At this time, the court acknowledges Ron Wilson is taking Ritalin, the most widely prescribed drug.

"The biofeedback technique was positively acclaimed by each person interviewed. Each stated the neurobiofeedback procedure was very helpful. Through the biofeedback techniques, each ADD victim had learned to affect the brain upon notice of an emotional state commencing. Each knew how to feed into their brain counter emotions and slow the brain's activity disrupting, afflictive emotions. It was referred to as the antidote procedure. Their example was the emotion impatience. The antidote for impatience was tolerance. As soon as impatience threatened to surface, the victim reacted and fed into the brain several tolerant thoughts, characteristics which released him of impatience. The ability for the brain to do this is due to the brain's plasticity. A recent discovery which refutes our historical belief that injured brain/nerve tissue cannot, will not repair itself, regenerate. The brain appears to exhibit plastic qualities. The brain will and can repair itself. It will develop new nerve routes and the brain will accept these. The brain's plasticity has benefited through biofeedback and it is a break-through treatment of ADD victims, among others."

The judge introduced quotes from "What's It Like to Have ADD," an article written by Dr. Edward M. Hollowell (copyright, 1992), and they appeared to be metaphors. The first, "It's like driving in the rain with bad windshield wipers, everything is smudged and blurred as you speed along and it's really frustrating not to see very well."

A second metaphor, "It's like listening to a radio station and a lot of static causes you to strain to hear what's going on." A third metaphor, "It's like trying to build a house of cards in a dust storm, you need to build a structure for yourself before you can ever start on the cards."

"I am now paraphrasing," said Judge Lowell. "From another ADD victim who he stated he felt supercharged much of the time. You get an idea and need to act upon it but here comes another idea before you have finished the first one. You drop the first idea and go to the second but here comes a third idea and it interrupts the second idea. Before you know it, you are categorized as impulsive and disorganized. You are trying hard all the time but these invisible ideas, often times many ideas, keep interrupting which makes it almost impossible to stay on task. You are so charged at times you seem to be spilling over constantly. Soon you are drumming your fingers, tapping your feet, twitching, whistling, singing, looking here, looking there, scratching and doodling. It appears you are not paying attention or not interested but you are spilling over so you *can* pay attention!

"ADD keeps you buzzing, being here and there and everywhere. Time verification is lost when suffering ADD. Time keeps everything from happening all at once. Time parcels moments into separate bits so that you can do one thing at a time. In ADD, this does not happen. It appears in ADD, time collapses. Time becomes a black hole. It feels as if everything happens all at once and creates a sense of inner turmoil or panic. ADD victims lose perspective and the ability to prioritize. They are constantly on the go, trying to keep the world from caving in on them.

"It appears that impatience is characteristic of all ADD patients. They are incapable of waiting in lines; impulse leads them to action. They are without the intermediate reflective stage. When an impulse fires into the brain, they must react immediately. They are not tactful; tact is reflecting on your words before speaking. These quick responses without thinking—just act—is the cause of tactlessness. ADD victims are not tactful.

"For an ADD sufferer, it takes a lot of effort and adapting to get on in life. But it certainly can be done and done well."

It was over. A most unusual sentencing lecture; however, required to enlighten people to the nature and requirements in the sentence. Ron Wilson had listened closely to Judge Lowell's remarks and, on occasion, it was observed Ron nodding his head in the affirmative and muttering, "Yup, that's me." It appeared Ron had to frequently fight back tears and Terrill, his attorney, had offered him his handkerchief.

Judge Lowell commenced, "Ron Wilson, you are sentenced to 25 years at Bridgeport Prison. After 12-1/2 years confinement, no longer, you will be paroled, if parole is warranted. Prison officials will be commanded to provide you the biofeedback programs and the qEEG analysis program. Before your release from Bridgeport Prison, they must supply this court data that the court will review and approve or reject parole. This court noticed you have not earned your high school diploma. The court will require a completed study curriculum at Bridgeport toward earning your high school diploma. It is essential you earn the diploma before you are paroled. This court encourages you, Mr. Wilson, to pursue a college degree upon your release from prison. Good luck. This court is adjourned."

Prison

The admitting office was Ron Wilson's initial contact with Bridgeport Prison. He was ushered into a receiving area and an officer briefed him on prison procedures. The daily prison routine was detailed for Ron: wake up time, lock down time, lights out time. This is referred to as orientation. Ron was required to work each day and he was told he would receive his work schedule within three days. He was also told he would be involved in what the official referred to as "finalizing" his enlightenment program, which referred to the court's directive for a biofeedback program to deal with Ron's ADD.

Ron was surprised and confused. *I did not expect in prison I would be able to have input into my development program. I thought prison dealt with punishment.*

Ron had a ray of hope for the future. He was grateful to Judge Lowell. The orientation officer explained he would be given a physical today. "You will strip bare and be subject to a required shake-down. Your body orifices will be examined for contraband drugs, and weapons. Prison clothing will be issued following your shower, shake-down. You dress into these. Also, bed clothing and pillow are issued along with your personal clothing. The first three days of imprisonment you will be housed in a segregated unit and will be the only person in a cell."

Later on his first day in prison, Ron would learn of the prison's rules and regulations. This is the imposed discipline behavior code. No will and choice, Ron would have his choices made for him. He had forsaken his gift of will and choice.

Ron had no doubt that Bridgeport Prison meant business and inmate discipline and behavior were priority commitments at Bridgeport Prison. Ron would comply with prison discipline and conduct codes. Consequences of misconduct were stern, swift, and a serious matter.

Except for lock-down, Ron was kept busy completing orientation. He did not have time to reflect on prison incarceration. Ron was looking forward to his work assignment. Would he have an opportunity to work at something he enjoyed? Included in his thoughts, when would he be able to start his high school studies and begin his ADD evaluation and treatment? Soon, he hoped and Ron was anxious but in a positive frame of mind.

Ron found time to reflect upon his trial. First Attorney Terrill came to mind and Ron was grateful for his attorney's efforts. The attorney had been very influential in obtaining a 25-year imprisonment sentence with parole after 12-1/2 years. Ron's attorney had exhibited compassion and strong interest in Ron. Interest displaying kindness, goodness, and sincere appreciation of a worthy being. Such attitude and behavior, Ron sighed, was the first kind behavior and attitude extended him. Judge Lowell's image flashed into Ron's mind. Ron's feelings for Judge Lowell were unusual, new, and not a routine feeling Ron had experienced. He felt kindness, fairness, and consideration toward Judge Lowell in return for the kindness, fairness, and consideration the judge had shown toward him. Ron was still unable to comprehend the judge's detailed interest in his illness, ADD. Ron felt he had been blessed and, with gratitude, said a thank you prayer. He felt no great obligation to either man, attorney or judge; he felt stronger emotions residing inside him. He felt sincerity, honesty, hopefulness, and diligence to do right. Yes, Ron had been directly in contact and influenced by two fine people whom he could count as advocates and friends: Attorney Terrill and Judge Lowell.

Ron was escorted to a small conference room. The officer he met was in charge of work assignments. The work director indicated some need for prison workers, and some urgent. He proceeded directly to the issue. "We have openings in the kitchen, workshop, library, and infirmary right now."

Ron was asked if he had any interest and experience in those areas. "Yes, I am interested in the library," Ron stated. The library had illuminated intentions in Ron's mind.

Ron asked, "What do I do in the library?"

The director asked the obvious but had been surprised in the past, "Can you read?" Ron replied, "Yes, I have scored high in reading."

The director had been closely observing Ron. With little information about Ron, he was trying to evaluate him. The director noticed Ron had dropped out of school in the tenth grade. He had school records showing an inconsistent achievement pattern, grade pattern. Finally, after the director's pause and eyeball evaluation he said, "You will be cataloging books as they are returned to the library." Ron had been assigned a job.

The fifth day of prison life, Ron was escorted to the prison's help-assessment department. He would be introduced to an assessment, evaluation, and diagnosis program, a program focused on rehabilitation from ADD.

The director began by telling Ron that he had been sent to his department upon request of the court. He noted that the biofeedback technique had a primary emphasis on the neurofeedback procedure. The director explained to Ron they were aware of earlier evaluation ordered by the court and the evaluation resulted in a diagnosis of ADD and ADOD. But it was required that they begin from the testing evaluation to support earlier diagnosis. Ron was familiar with the tests he had already experienced and was not excited about having to do them again, but this was a new start, a new outlook for the future. He knew he would eventually be free. Ron was satisfied and he would cooperate to the fullest.

Information the director employed in neurofeedback techniques and brain wave description was obtained directly from a visitation with Robert L. Gurnee, MSW, CISW in his Attention Deficit Disorder clinic.

The director introduced Ron to the neurofeedback technique as the primary technique which would monitor Ron's electrical brain activity. This test would indicate different patterns of brain waves and the waves' frequency accompanying emotions. The neurofeedback procedure would record any peculiarity in the brain's waves. Negative, destructive emotions would register extra strength and greater frequency waves recording information useful in treating Ron. The director used a quantitative electroencephalography measuring the electrical activity of the cerebral cortex of the brain. qEEG, brain mapping measures electrical patterns at the surface of the scalp. The measurement records cortical electrical activity or brain waves, the frequencies of the brain must be known. Delta waves are the slowest, highest amplitude waves. These waves occur during sleep. Delta activity during the waking state is considered pathological and represents something wrong. The Theta waves have a higher and lower range. The lower range Theta waves represent the twilight zone between waking and sleep. This is a calm and serene state. At the lower Theta range very little intellectual activity occurs. Higher range Theta waves are recognized when the brain is engaging in complex, focused problem solving, as in arithmetic.

Alpha brain waves are slower frequency and higher amplitude. Alpha waves indicate the brain is relaxing and indicates the brain is shifting into idle, relaxed, and disengaged, waiting to respond when needed. Alpha is associated with complex tasks. Finally, Beta brain waves are low amplitude, higher frequency (faster) brain waves associated with a state of mental, intellectual activity and outwardly focused attention or concentration. Everyone has some of each brain wave bands present in different regions of the cerebral cortex.

Here are examples of individuals' state of brain waves. While sleeping, there are more Delta and slow Theta brainwaves. During inattentiveness or daydreaming, there are more Theta and sometimes low frequency Alpha present. Anxiety and tenseness produce excessively high frequency Beta. A person suffering with obsessive-compulsive disorder will have excessive high frequency, Beta activity. To summate, sufferers from ADD likely have excessive slow waves, usually Delta, slow Theta, and sometimes excessively low frequency Alpha. Unusual slow wave action in the frontal part of the cerebral cortex promotes difficulty controlling attention and emotions. This causes serious problems with concentration, memory, impulse control, and mood shifts, or hyperactivity.

The director informed Ron his test results indicated he had excessive slow wave activity in his cerebral cortex. The presence of these slow waves decreases concentration, loss of attention, poor memory, mood shifts, and impulsiveness. The biofeedback information and background intended to help Ron understand the need for treatment and what the treatment could do to help Ron. The director was positive and well informed and Ron intended to cooperate and benefit from the program.

Accompanying the director was a therapist, Marvin, and he would be the chief therapist working with Ron. Marvin was asked to explain the antidote program. The background for the antidote program which was 10 years new, was based on research. Brain research provided exciting, beneficial news. Previously it was fact that brain cell tissue damage, loss resulted in little or no regeneration of damaged, lost tissue. But recent research demonstrated brain tissue will regenerate new cell fields. The research provided the plasticity quality of the brain. Plasticity of the brain permits a dynamacy in the brain for acquiring and expanding thoughts. The brain accepts new concepts, ideas which replace old concepts and permits amending of a destructive thought.

ADD victims are impatient, can't stand to wait, can't stand in line, they do not display any degree of patience. Due to the brain's receptive plasticity, one can teach/learn an antidote such as tolerance to replace impatience. Tolerance technique is taught/learned and the ADD victim replaces impatience with tolerance and learns to think tolerantly. Several tolerant thoughts are nurtured and focused with attention resulting in tolerant behavior. The brain will adjust and shift gears from impatience to tolerance with practice and proper training. Anger is a common destructive, emotion. An antidote to substitute for anger, is loving kindness. The plasticity quality of the brain accepts many new thoughts through meditation. You train your mind to meditate and diffuse unfavorable emotions, such as anger, and supplement thoughts with a positive antidote. The positive antidote, loving kindness, replaces the destructive emotion, angry thoughts. As you meditate and employ the resiliency of a plastic brain, you replace destructive, fixed thoughts and emotions with positive thoughts beneficial for the individual."

The therapist, Marvin, was speaking directly to Ron. "Upon review of background information, we have determined to begin your rehab, concentrating on removing anger." *Just like that, remove anger,* Ron thought. A highly positive goal it was. Reducing some anger in Ron would suffice. "Ron, your background information indicates you have a strong attachment with anger. Anger is a basic, broad emotion in all of us but fortunately some can control their anger—while, unfortunately others cannot."

"We would like you to be able to understand anger and where it originates Anger can serve both good and bad; however, we are focusing upon negative anger. Anger springs from resentment and resentment leads to revenge and is very dangerous. Anger as a lifestyle is explosive and angry persons are usually irritable, fly-off-the handle people who are easily slighted and insulted. They become bullies, fighters. Anger stems from wants. We exaggerate the importance for worldly desire. Next we become frustrated because we cannot satisfy all our wants or desires. Unsatisfied desires cause people to go into rage, just like a baby who desires but can't tell you what it is he/she desires. Finally, anger leads to hate. Hate is so potent it affects all facets of an individual's life. Ron, we are commencing with anger since it overflows into many other deleterious emotions and feelings: resentment, hate, and frustration. Anger is behind many homicides, suicides, and wars.

"We will explain the refractory period and help you recognize it as well as employ it. The refractory period is a short period of time between the onset of the emotion you recognize is coming. The gap between the impulse and before your response is called the refractory period. The antidote technique is applied during the refractory period. And more, anger, an undesirable emotion, will be replaced by loving thoughts, loving kindness. This diffuses the anger. All negative emotions can be removed by the alternate antidote technique."

Ron was very interested and observant. He heard it all and he applied it all to himself. He wanted to be rid of all his impulsive, nasty thoughts resulting in nasty emotions and he thought, *Could this be what I have been looking for?* He would do his very best and he would cooperate. Could he return to society a happy person and become successful? He told himself yes.

The therapist wanted to impress on Ron the antidote idea again. He told Ron to observe that for each emotion there was an opposite antidote. He stated, "Light is the opposite of dark. Hate's opposite is love, etc. We play the imagination word game. Select any word and imagine the word with all your thoughts and create new images for the word and then select an antidote-alternate. View the opposite word with your power of imagination and associate the word-thoughts with your experience. You are employing your third eye, the eye of imagination. Employing your imagination you can implant positive meaning into your life and abandon negative, destructive thoughts and emotions. You have the means to choose the positive, constructive thoughts and emotions. The imagination mind word game is a powerful asset you can implement at any and all times." This had been a very good learning experience and Ron felt he would benefit greatly.

The Bridgeport Prison warden was a strong pro-education leader. W. D. Walters. Superintendent Walters had implemented some innovative programs during his term. One of the most aggressive programs was the self-help educational program. The educational program's primary objective was to assist the prisoners in obtaining their high school diploma. The post-high school program led to obtaining an AA (Associate of Arts) degree. Its motive was to prepare the prisoner for greater job opportunities after release from Bridgeport Prison.

The ability to advance their education appealed to many prisoners. The Warden and staff knew the opportunity to learn and better oneself was a strong motivator and they felt it contributed to better behavior by the prisoners. Discipline was strong but fair at Bridgeport Prison and W. D. Walters felt the educational opportunity the institution offered had an effect. The primary concept W. D. Walters experienced was rehabilitation. The Warden felt strongly incarceration, as a penalty must be a power in the enhancement of the individual prisoner. Incarceration must assist in a positive enlightenment, evaluation of the prisoner. Prison programs must raise the prisoner's consciousness by replacing destructive thoughts with constructive thoughts.

During lock up, Ron had a visitor. It was Donald West, the educational counselor. He came to visit Ron and help Ron set up his educational curriculum. The counselor set a meeting for Ron to visit his office. They would review Ron's record pertaining to his formal school attendance. Mr. West would help Ron with a short-goal and a long-goal phase. The counselor was experienced and knew the importance of some early success-achievement; therefore, the necessity of a short-goal program. Donald West's meeting with Ron ended on a high note.

In the short time Ron had been in Bridgeport Prison, he had experienced one-on-one consultations that were friendly and very informative. He had never had such concentrated attention paid him or attention sincerely directed to helping him. In his lifetime he had never shared the kindness, goodness, and love he shared with his attorney, Mr. Terrill, and Judge Lowell. And at Bridgeport he was again feeling the same emotions. These were the positive feelings necessary to turn his life around.

Time Passes

Serving time is what you make of it. Wherever and whatever your situation, you can be productive and functional as a human being. You can exist to learn and improve as a human or you can exist merely to die and escape any responsibility. Ron had benefited from a surge in enthusiasm that raised his goals. He had acquired momentum for life from his trial experience and had benefited already at Bridgeport from professional dedication to education. He wanted to learn and become somebody. The first step toward fulfilling his goal was to learn about his emotions and feelings. He wanted to acquire control of his own behavior. Perhaps the biofeedback program could help him do so. What was it that caused his brain to function improperly permitting strong negative emotions and feelings to occur without any control? Perhaps the qEEG program would determine the brain malfunctions when certain emotions and feelings occur. And perhaps the antidote substitution maneuver could control negative emotions and feelings.

Ron had applied his early teachings for his benefit and he was motivated to carry through. He would learn how the brain controlled the specific behaviors that were at the center of ADD illness. The very promise of releasing himself from his negative characteristics while in Bridgeport Prison supplied him with energy and enthusiasm for what was ahead.

Ron would pass time in prison studying for his high school diploma. He liked Marvin, his teacher/counselor, and determined Marvin would contribute to his educational goal. Ron convinced himself of the necessity for an education so he could function effectively in society upon his release from prison. He wanted stability in life, and stability would be grounded in education. He was very grateful to serve the sentence at Bridgeport because time would pass in self-improvement, reformed behavior, and education. Improved self control, behavior, and a higher education are essential to live and function successfully in society.

Ron suffered the loss of his mother, Elsie, early in his prison term. She died from a massive heart attack. Elsie had been a chronic hypertension person throughout and she had not managed her health care wisely. Ron was grateful his mother died immediately and did not suffer long disability. Ron was alone. Ron could not help but reflect upon his mother. He loved her. She was his mother but he would move on alone as he had always done. His love for his mother was a love out of respect for motherhood. He respected his mother for her courage and efforts to raise him. He respected his mother for dealing with the hopelessness of his father, Glen. He wondered and was curious about his father. He had not seen or heard from Glen since he left home. Where was his father? Was he dead, in jail or was he another number, derelict on the street, existing?

He returned to the present. He was in Bridgeport Prison but still he felt a degree of hopelessness on the one hand and a degree of inspiration too. Had he been incarcerated at State Prison, he would be handling the usual prison routine and serving some hard time. But he was only 20 years of age with a future before him, and Bridgeport Prison would be a major part of that future.

W. D. Walters, the prison superintendent, had lobbied for a new, unique enlightenment program. The Warden was able to gain support from the parole board and in turn the state legislature. The program had been granted. For years, sociologists and psychologists had been pioneering self-improvement programs for institutionalized persons. Prisoners did not need hard time, they did not need excessive penalties, prisoners needed programs to help them prepare for their return into society. Most prisoners leave prison in due time. This was the wave of sentiment and W. D. Walters jumped on its wagon. He was grateful because his philosophy was pro-self improvement programs, innovated and rehabilitated programs based on education for self-improvement.

Underlying concepts of the Bridgeport program were increasing awareness of oneself, the world, and higher consciousness. *Who am I? Why do I act as I do?* Insight into answering these questions would benefit Ron in understanding his nature and understanding the nature of others. *What is the real world? What world am I in?* Insight answering these questions would benefit Ron to understand that the world he had functioned in was not the real world; *or was it the only world?* He has an opportunity to choose his world reality because of the gift, Divine Will. Because of W. D. Walters' wisdom and efforts to implement enlightenment, educational programs, Ron Wilson among many prisoners could improve their lives.

W. D. Walters based his efforts for approval of his program on several new research studies. The basis of the research was to determine the effects of negative emotions, (e.g., anger, etc.) and positive emotions, (e.g., love, etc.) on consciousness.

These studies discovered that indicator muscles would strengthen in response to positive stimuli, (e.g., love) and indicator muscles would weaken in response to negative stimuli, (e.g., anger). Since a smile is a positive stimulus, it tests strong; a frown is a negative stimulus, it tests weak. Several studies have been conducted based on truth or lie. Telling the truth is a positive quality of consciousness and speaking the truth will cause indicator muscles to contract, be strong. Telling a lie, which is a consciously negative quality, causes the indicator muscles to go weak and limp.

The result of this is that we can determine the truth or the lie for all individuals. Anyone's thoughts and emotional state can be tested regarding the person's level of consciousness. It can measure levels of consciousness for all facets of life, e.g., work, play, study, etc. The levels of consciousness of the ill, sick, criminal, impoverished, healthy, and successful persons can be measured.

The study of kinesiology is ancient. It studies the reaction and movement of muscles responding to various stimuli first observed in conditioning and physical training. Recent research has studied and calibrated the effects of various stimuli: emotions, hate, anger, joy, and love regarding effects of emotions in the consciousness of the person. Muscle reactions to various emotions were calibrated and found; for example, muscle responds weak in presence of lies etc. and responds strong in presence of truth, etc.

After twenty-plus years of study and research, Dr. David Hawkins learned an explosive truth if employed with purity of heart and purest intentions would redefine our world from a negative world, crime and war, a negative consciousness into a world of love and peace, a positive consciousness. He created a method of calibrating the truth with a range of 1 to 1,000. This study of consciousness produced a calibrated profile of the entire human condition, permitting an analysis of the emotional and spiritual make-up of individuals, societies, and the human race.

The consciousness and awareness of prisoners needed improvement through education and spiritual enlightenment. Much would be gained by the prisoner and his fellow prisoners as well as all mankind if the individual could have a new awakening. Awaken to the worth of self and others and a real awareness to great opportunity in their world. Can the prisoner's fragile and flighty mind be identified as mind and Ego—one and the same?

Yes, Warden W. D. Walters' belief was prisoners are asleep, mesmerized by negatives and prisoners must become awake, aware. The prisoner must think new thoughts about himself, others, and the world in which he lives. It is worth the effort to try to awaken the prisoner and enlighten him about himself and society. Possibly he might respond, change, and move into society functioning in a new consciousness. But the Warden surmised it would be a difficult task based on the prisoner's Ego and dedication of his mind and body toward wants and desires, worldly goods. As difficult a task as it was, Warden W. D. Walters knew that improvement would manifest itself if one, just one, prisoner benefited and lived successfully and happily in society. Can we distinguish for each prisoner in our enlightenment program the necessity for separating their desires and wants from their needs? If this had occurred earlier in the life of each prisoner and tolerance had been substituted for impatience, perhaps the prisoner would not be in Bridgeport and would not have resorted to crime. Desires and wants turn people to crime since they become very impatient and intolerant resulting in theft, burglary, muggings, and murder; the result of a runaway Ego/mind's illusionary world.

W. D. Walters, a renowned critic of labor camps, also

referred to as prisons where little consideration was given the inmates other than turning incorrigibles to be even more corruptible. W. D. was the instigator, author of humane treatment for prisoners and creator of hope for those incarcerated. The incarcerated called him "Savior." The Warden perceived the world not as the Ego/mind perceives it but as a gracious giver, provider of all our needs. He detested the illusionary Ego's belief that the world owes me what I desire and want but that's what he determined his destiny to be. Work is an illusionary scenario and he attempted to help his guests change the scene. Prisoners, he claimed, have runaway Egos and are constantly riding a merry-go-around. They go in circles but never get anywhere.

W. D. Walters' summation of the prisoner's Ego/mind illusionary self: "He is always right, everyone else is wrong and everyone else is the cause for his demise. He sees himself as a 'big fish' and sometimes the only fish in society. I am 'uno,' number one. He loves the Ego/mind partnership and his fears of death are only present when he doesn't satisfy the Ego's selfish demands. He fears the Ego will kill him so he must find ways and means to satisfy the Ego even when it means death, but death to others—murder. He sees himself as the sum total of all his possessions, so possess he must. *I never have enough and I can never get enough of my sick mind's demand.* The Ego/mind poisons him. He deprives himself of basic needs, e.g., food, water, and medicine in order to satisfy the Ego/mind's illusionary desires, wants. His perception prohibits knowing who he is or where he originated. He is debris treating himself as manure but is salvageable.

"However; we must at least try as he is our brother and we must look after our brothers. The best way is show him love, kindness, peace, and contentment. He is no different than we, he has a self but is lost in the sick world; the world perception has created with the Ego."

W. D. Walters had focused his innovative enlightenment program on identification. Identification of oneself was one's world as it really is. He subjects inmates to an evaluation of awareness and consciousness with clear daylight and each prisoner sees the calibration of his emotions and feelings. The tool he uses for awareness is the calibrated kinesiological test. "I want to assist the prisoners in evaluation of self by becoming more aware and raising their consciousness level."

It is interesting to learn the energy calibrations of the emotions, feelings included in the kinesiological research study. The lowest energy shame calibrated at 20; guilt 30; apathy 50; grief 75; fear 100; anger 150; pride 175; courage 200; neutrality 250; willingness 310; acceptance 350; reason 400; love 500; joy 540; peace 600; and enlightenment 700–1000.

An individual testing 20 is near physical death and many suicides result due to shame, a pathetic existence. Anger scores 150 and includes frustrated persons whose desires and wants manifest anger. Anger originates from exaggerating the importance of desires, wants. Angry persons may advance into rage, as any child does. Anger leads to hatred and many causes produce anger. Courage at 200 on the scale is very significant. Courage is the break-even point between negative and positive energy fields. Courage is the point which provides a degree of integrity, truth. A score of 200 or greater on the scale represents a positive, beneficial existence whereas a score lower than 200 on the scale represents a negative; troubled, destructive existence. It is interesting to learn that less than 20 years ago the population of the United States tested 197, below the break-even score, below the positive emergence point. In the last 10 years, the score has risen to 207, Amen! Even more alarming is that less than 20% of the positive testing population carried, supported, enhanced the entire negative population. More alarming still, several hundred sayers, mystics, highly enlightened persons supported and compensated for the low disempowering multitudes. How powerful positive thoughts promoting feelings of love, peace, and charity are when a very small percentage of people can carry the entire world's population. The destructiveness of negative thoughts and emotions: anger, fear, guilt, lies, and cheating, etc., is the cause of crime, murder, and wars. When power versus force, God's power always wins versus the devil's force. As Ron Wilson prepared to participate in Warden W. D. Walters' enlightenment program, Ron would become a happier more productive person and would empower others as well as himself.

Love at 500 calibrations is characterized as permanent. It does not fluctuate; its source does not rely on the external forces. Loving is a state of being. Love is not intellectualized and does not proceed from the end; love comes from the heart. Love is inclusive and enlarges the sense of self. Love represents true happiness. And enlightenment calibrated at 700/1000 represents the calibration of our great thinkers, teachers, and spiritual leaders. This group includes the great Avatars (Lords: Lord Krishna; Lord Buddha, and our Lord Jesus Christ. Few rise to this level of enlightenment, spirituality.

W. D. Walters' goal for the enlightenment program was to target a calibration of 200 break-even or more for each prisoner in the program. It must increase individual prisoner's awareness and increase each prisoner's consciousness. If this could be achieved, W. D. Walters knew the entire prison population, staff, and administrators' empowering energy field would rise also. Every human is positively affected.

Ron Wilson completed his fourth year in the enhancement program. Anger had been the principal negative emotion, so Ron concentrated his efforts and energy on anger. He must learn what caused his anger and he must learn how to control anger. He felt he had improved in dealing with anger. Anger control benefited Ron in other ways. Anger grows and results in several other negative emotions as resentment and revenge. A vicious cycle results with anger caught on a merry-go-round and other negative emotions lead to anger and some negative emotions result from anger.

Ron was in a reflective mood. He was recalling things he had learned. Today he was reviewing what he learned and knew about the Ego. He had never heard of the Ego before and he had never associated the mind with Ego. He was surprised to learn that the mind and the Ego were one and the same. It remained a puzzle for him and he had difficulty understanding the idea that the Ego is an illusion of the mind from his perception. He had trouble realizing his perception would be wrong. He understood perception to be how he saw things and his thoughts pertaining to what he saw. If he saw it, how could it be wrong? Ron was told his faulty projection caused his false perception. You project from within what you want to project to the outside and this is what you perceive.

Ron had been instructed how to project favorably by viewing the world for what it is, an evil world as he perceived it. He had not held this concept before his enlightenment program experience. Ron had not understood, but did now, that other persons did not perceive the world as he did. He had grasped the concept that perception varied from individual to individual. He had been introduced to the concept the Ego influenced his mind and identified him as an image of the world and all its worldly possessions: money, cars, home, etc. He had been told that the Ego was never satisfied and, consequently, was the driving force behind all his desires and wants for worldly possessions and pleasure. Egotists identified with worldly possessions and these possessions were their identity.

When Ron questioned Marvin about ending this craziness and questioned how long can it go, he was told as long as you do not distinguish your desires and wants from your needs. It continues as long as you are willing to pay the price, e.g., frustration, fear, and anger, a severe price that can lead to crime and murder. When Ron heard this, he was astonished to think his egoism had possibly precipitated murder. But it appears it played a part. He wanted to know how he could end his harmful craving; so he asked, "How can I stop my cravings, desires, and wants?" He was told he must identify his real self from his worldly self. The counselor referred the worldly self as the "little self" and his "Real Self" as the "Larger Self." Marvin added that the difference between the two selves is that the "Little Self" is external and without your body and the "Larger Self" is within. Ron puzzled, quickly added, "Where is my real self, Larger Self?" And again he was told this self lies within your Spirit, Soul, and heart.

Ron was really confused and told his counselor, "I am not aware of my Spirit and Soul within me but I know I have a heart." He was sincere and clinging to hope that he might learn about his Spirit and Soul.

The counselor did not hesitate and he began, "Ron, your awareness of self, the real you, and your consciousness is enlightened through your Spirit and Soul. The Spirit and Soul reveal what you believe in your heart to be evident, true. You are a son of God, as we all are, and not the son of an illusionary, worldly God, a God of make-believe."

Ron followed some of this but he remained confused and hoped for further enlightenment pertaining to his "Larger Self," and his "Real Self."

In the end, the therapist said, "Ron, your Real Self does not want for anything, you have no desire and wants because you need not, your needs are provided by a higher Power. Ron, the Larger Self deals not in desires and wants from the world since the Larger Self is without an Ego which pushes, shoves, tricks, and maneuvers you through lies. The Larger Self is at peace and enjoys everything in his world: people, animals, flowers, trees, water, clouds in the sky. These are very empowering and provide great energizing thoughts of beauty, peace, love, and contentment."

Ron was staring ahead absorbed in self-indulgent thoughts. Perhaps he was disturbed with the Ego/mind games? Ron was agitated and he could not learn fast enough. "Again, how do I become aware of my Larger Self and aware of the real world?"

The counselor responded, "You are commencing to learn within the context of our discussion. And, as your Spirit and Soul cause you to realize you are not a make-believe, illusionary Ego, a make-believe little self, our awareness and consciousness provide the detail."

Ron would cherish the ability to put an end to his cravings. He sensed he was two persons in one, his little self and his Larger Self, and the little self was responsible for his cravings. He had advanced to this level of awareness and sensed there was some mysterious person concealed inside him. He needed to discover this stranger.

He broke away from the train of thought and asked,

"Is the Ego responsible for my impatience, frustration, and anger?"

"Absolutely, the Ego causes your desires and wants which lead to anger."

"Is this the manner in which my Ego/mind affects my consciousness? And what is consciousness and where can I find it?"

The counselor said to himself, we are certainly progressing since his curiosity wants to know.

The counselor said, "Consciousness is universal, worldwide, everywhere, you name it. And it is the source of knowledge, truth, and wisdom and has high energy. Consciousness is available for everyone. Whoever uses it does so from individual consciousness. Individual consciousness has energy of its own and energy is fueled by our beliefs, emotions. When you employ positive beliefs, positive emotions provide good results, feelings and are to your benefit and that of mankind. This makes for a high level of consciousness. In this positive mood, you have great energy for accessing, if you desire, more energy leading to greater belief, knowledge and wisdom from within the vast universe."

The therapist paused then continued, "Ron, universal awareness and consciousness is like a great database. The universal database has beliefs, concepts, knowledge, truth, and wisdom; everything is here and available to anyone. Everything known, accomplished, and achieved throughout time in the universe is here and available. And you Ron, your consciousness is a part of the universal consciousness. In reality there is no truth, knowledge, and wisdom unknown. It's found in the universal consciousness but each person to benefit from this information needs to access it.

"Ron, I emphasize again, consciousness is everywhere and consciousness is everything, e.g., knowledge, truth, and wisdom, etc."

Ron was absorbing as much of this as possible for now and would need to reflect, think about what he had heard.

Then Marvin said, "To answer your question, how does your Ego/mind affect your consciousness? Your awareness and consciousness of the 'Larger Self' is lowered by the Ego/mind and the 'little self' is perceived more important. Through your projections of how you perceive your world, the little self becomes the servant of the ruler Ego/mind. The Ego/mind causes great thirst and demand for desires and wants of a worldly nature: money, cars, clothes, homes, and all material things you perceive useful and of value to enhance your stature. Look, if I can acquire this and that, I am somebody! This is who I am! The Ego/mind manifests the little self and it rules the roost. Your awareness and consciousness of your Real Self 'Larger Self' lies dormant within you."

The counselor looked at Ron and paused, waiting for a response. He had a response from Ron but it was not verbal. It was a response so unbelievable. How can this be, but do tell me more!

The therapist sensed as much from Ron and asked, "Ron, this is a very vicious cycle, your make-believe world, caused by wrong projections, error in perceptions, and engineered by your Ego/mind through your little self. It goes on 100% of the time never deserting the willing participant. Because of burning desires and wants and many not obtainable, great frustration, anger, and even crime—yes murder ensues. It grows and spreads like a wild fire, a forest fire and destroys. Your consciousness is controlled by your command; it goes along with your make-believe game. The consciousness is focused on getting this, getting that, and other wants. The Ego/mind assures you this is proper behavior to get places and be somebody but it is totally incorrect, disempowering behavior. Your energy, what little you have, is employed to satisfy your desires and wants and you are unable to, or desire not to, draw positive energy from the universal source, your source. Both the Ego/mind demands for more and more, never enough, continues and eventually all energy is gone. No energy to think positively, no energy to determine right from wrong. Eventually all energy is negative and you are totally disempowered. But your wants and desires spread as a forest fire. Finally, the negative thoughts prevail and crime results. You lie, cheat, steal, and kill to meet your desires and wants. A real friend, the one who tells you he is your friend, Ego/mind, soon deserts you. You cannot satisfy worldly desires and wants while incarcerated. You are the loser of a make-believe game and your Ego/mind is the winner since he always destroys, kills."

The counselor then suggested they end today's discussion.

"No," Ron blurted out. "I want to know of the 'little self' and 'Larger Self.'"

Marvin, the head therapist, stated, "I want to discuss your 'little self' and 'Larger Self' dilemma you are struggling with as many do."

Marvin continued, "Ron, think in terms of two selves, the 'little self' and the 'Larger Self!' The little self is the realization that you are involved in the Ego/mind's worldly game. I, myself, permit me to participate and this self is one that I am. Your Larger Self is not connected and involved in the world's games or the Ego/mind's shenanigans. The Larger Self divorces itself from your body, the body that carries out the Ego/mind's commands and wishes. The Larger Self is removed from body functions and is the direct product of your spirit-soul. It is associated with Divine Reality. The Larger Self is that part of you that enjoys benefits from your Spiritual Consciousness, e.g., creation, love, kindness, joy, happiness, and contentment, etc. Contrast this with your 'little self' playing the Ego/mind's worldly games, e.g., shame, guilt, fear, anger, and other negative emotions, feelings."

Ron had little difficulty grasping the antidote program. He enjoyed the word, emotion-feelings game. His recognition of overpowering negative thoughts and emotions and his new-found word thoughts substitution technique had improved his disposition and contributed to a calmer and more serene personality. He recognized this much and besides he recognized he had improved his vocabulary. He enjoyed searching his dictionary for appropriate substitute words. A primary focus of the word game was to convert or eliminate negative words and thoughts in his consciousness into positive words and thoughts into his consciousness. The result was to stop negative feelings and create positive feelings. Ron could control some frustration and anger with this technique. The brain's plasticity permitted new thought patterns to occur and permit voluntary injection of new words and thoughts in replacement of old words and thoughts.

Ron's attorney came to visit Ron. Early in their visit, the conversation turned to the enhancement program. Attorney Terrill asked Ron which part of the program benefited him the most.

Ron replied, "The antidote program."

Mr. Terrill asked Ron how this program worked. Ron said, "I can detect, feel when a thought will produce a negative feeling prior to the onset of the feeling/emotion. At this instant is a refractory period which is that brief time between a stimulus and actual feeling. It is called the refractory period."

Attorney Terrill recognized that emotionally healthy persons employ the refractory period automatically; however the surmised overly reactive, irrational persons probably lack this technique but can be taught it, as apparently Ron is.

Then Ron continued, "I have been taught to substitute a new word, 'antidote,' during the refractory period and this replaces the negative word, feeling about to occur."

Ron was pleased with his effort to explain the technique but wanted to make certain Mr. Terrill understood the exact mechanics involved. Ron continued, "Mr. Terrill, as you know, the word resentment is very negative and when I feel resentment enter into my consciousness, I insert an antidote, replacement. I have learned new words with opposite feelings. I might use the thought acceptance as my antidote for resentment. Acceptance is a positive thought and I have trained my mind to think positive so the mind accepts the new empowering thought. I am no longer resentful and besides my former resentment would turn into rage, revenge. So by the antidote technique, I stay free of many negative thoughts and feelings. I have found with help from my dictionary which tells me that every negative word has an antidote." Although Terrill was very impressed and pleased and said, "Ron, I need some of that therapy." Ron smiled and felt achievement. Is that a positive word-feeling or must he rush to his dictionary in search of an antidote? Never, it would turn out negative.

Parole and After

Ron had completed his high school diploma. He achieved a 3.0 GPA (Grade Point Average). In addition, he successfully completed three lower level college courses. He studied business finance and planned to enter a four-year college to earn a B.A. (Bachelor of Arts) degree in business finance. Upon parole from Bridgeport Prison, he decided to pursue a business career.

The prison had a parolee's assistance department primarily to assist parolees with job procurement. Ron had been offered a position in a retail business. The position was contingent upon Ron earning a B.A. degree within a period of four years from the time of employment. A final reflection as Ron awaited parole was that he acquired a greater awareness of himself and the world he would live in and he improved his consciousness for life where his Real Self, 'Larger Self' could direct him.

Ron Wilson was thirty-two years of age when paroled from Bridgeport Prison. He had served twelve years and been granted parole six months early.

Ron's attorney, Mr. Terrill, remained a friend and helper while Ron was in prison. He attended to many pre-parole details. Terrill had been instrumental in Ron's job procurement. The attorney located housing in a quiet middle class neighborhood close to Cleveland Gear Company, his employer.

Mr. Terrill entered Bridgeport Prison at 12:45 P.M. He went directly to the main office and seated in this office was Ron. Mr. Terrill pulled to a halt for a few seconds and glanced at Ron; he broke into a smile. Ron greeted Mr. Terrill with a sincere embrace and breathed, "It is over, on with life."

Ron had been processed for release and had a duffel bag containing his possessions, clothes, and toiletries. In his pocket was a check for $1,300 saved in prison, representing his liquid assets. His friend, an attorney, secured a $2,500 loan for Ron. Ron's savings and the loan would provide funds to begin life anew. He felt solvent and appreciative of Mr. Terrill and all his efforts. Tomorrow he would deposit $1,300 received from the prison, and with the $2,500 loan; he would have $3,800.

Ron felt jubilant about his liberty and this blessed day and was joyfully looking ahead to a new life. However, he had a slight knot in his stomach as he momentarily reflected on his past. He reflected, *I am thirty-two years of age and without stature in society.* But he noted with confidence, *I will do my best and reward myself and everyone who helped me get to this day, primarily Mr. Terrill.* Ron felt a father-son relationship with Mr. Terrill, a relationship he had not previously experienced.

Ron Wilson and Mr. Terrill departed the prison. They crossed the street into a guest parking lot and got into Mr. Terrill's car. As they pulled out of the parking lot and away from Bridgeport, Ron and Mr. Terrill clasped hands. That was it, no more. Ron would not need to return to the prison because his parole office was in the government office downtown. Ron would visit monthly his parole officer for the first year and bimonthly, six times a year the second year, and twice a year the third year. His parole was three years with strict compliance. Ron intended to fulfill his parole obligation with a positive attitude. He looked forward to meeting his parole officer and hoped the officer would be fair and honest.

En route uptown to Rosewell Street, Ron's new home, Mr. Terrill and Ron had little conversation. It was obvious they were being reflective and conscious that Ron had come full circle, prisoner to free man. Finally, Mr. Terrill broke the silence saying, "Ron, this will be different, new, and very challenging for you. I have confidence you will do fine as you have since I have known you. Ron, I am very proud of you and want to remain close with you. Be sure to stay in contact with me."

Ron was very thoughtful, very pleased, very happy, and felt the security and contentment as a son and father would while bonding with love and friendship.

They were on Rosewell Street and looking for 102 Rosewell Street, Ron's new home. Mr. Terrill spotted the house. Ron felt apprehensive. What if his landlord didn't like him and how would the landlord accept a former con? It was premature to postulate relationship ideas and problems before meeting the landlord. He quickly released his apprehension and fear, negative feelings, with an antidote of kindness. He thought of the landlord positively, kind, and gracious. He would not permit disempowering words and thoughts to enter his consciousness. He was grateful for this lesson learned in Bridgeport. Good can come from confinement if you allow it—and Ron was allowing it.

Mr. Terrill rang the doorbell and waited for a response. A pleasant, plump lady opened the door and greeted them. Mrs. Agnes Robinson introduced herself and escorted them into the living room. She explained that her husband, Mel Robinson, was at work. She informed her guests that her husband had worked at Cleveland Gear Co. for fifteen years.

Ron was surprised and informed the landlady, that

he would be working for Cleveland Gear Co. beginning Monday morning at 8:00 A.M.

Agnes escorted them to Ron's living quarters which consisted of a small kitchen, living room, bedroom, and bathroom. It was small but basic and Ron knew it would be fine. The landlady told Ron if there was anything he needed, to call downstairs. He said he would do so and thanked her.

Agnes excused herself and Ron and Mr. Terrill were alone in Ron's new home.

Mr. Terrill suggested they go to the bank and deposit Ron's money. The attorney suggested Ron could unpack and settle in later. "After we visit the bank, we will go over to Cleveland Gear Co. so you can finalize employment details."

Ron was preparing for a meeting with the banker and his boss. He prepared himself by saying, "I know my banker and boss are both friendly and will be kind and considerate." He was ingesting positive words and positive feelings before any negative emotions could arrive. He would provide himself a positive start with positive, empowering, high-energy feelings.

Things proceeded like clockwork at the bank and Cleveland Gear Co. and everything transpired smoothly. Following their visit to Cleveland Gear Co., Ron advised Mr. Terrill he would like to walk the short distance to his home at 102 Rosewell Street. They parted here.

Ron has worked for Cleveland Gear Co. for four months. He was assigned to the purchasing department working on inventory control. He made inventory purchases and kept the inventory account balance. It was a satisfactory assignment. Ron was working in his field of interest. He planned to enter City College and pursue a business finance degree.

At City College he enrolled in two evening courses on Tuesday and Thursday from 6:00 P.M. to 9:00 P.M. City College had awarded Ron credit for credits he earned at Bridgeport Prison. His projected course was arranged so that he would complete requirements for his Business Finance Degree in 3 1/2 years. This was within the four-year time limit set by his probation. Ron worked each day diligently at his job and studied hard by night. He had a considerable amount of reading and research required for course work so he spent his evenings in the City College Library.

Fellow employees at Cleveland Gear Co. were good people. His department had quality, capable employees who were willing to teach Ron the department's methods and procedures. He accepted their help graciously. Alex was Ron's supervisor. Alex noted early Ron was a very willing student and learned quickly. Alex felt Ron had a good future in the company and hoped Ron would continue to work hard since Alex wanted to retain him. He could foresee a bright future for Ron with Cleveland Gear Co.

The classes at City College were difficult and time consuming. Outside of class, research and papers were required. Ron spent Monday, Wednesday, and Friday evenings in the City College Library. The schedule allowed him some free time on the weekends. His grades were good because he was faithful to his schedule.

One evening in the library, Ron met a very dedicated student, Elaine, who was on a crash course in Sociology. She had a full time job and was also attending City College evenings. Both Elaine and Ron had busy school schedules and their job commitments left them with little free time, but Ron felt the need of a social life and he felt

Elaine could use some distraction from her unrelenting schedule of work.

Ron and Elaine became close friends and spent much time discussing life goals. Elaine was from a small rural town and dreamed about going to the city and becoming somebody. She came from a poor family, but a close family that worked hard and was devoted to one another. Her hometown offered little opportunity for employment with future promotions. The salaries were minimal and hardly above minimum wage. Elaine was determined to overcome her background and improve her station in life. She wanted to help her parents improve their stations in life, as well.

Ron listened to Elaine's family story and yearned for a similar background. He told Elaine about his childhood in another city. He described his family and their dysfunction. He told it all, truthfully—about having been convicted of murder and the resultant twelve years at Bridgeport Prison. He told Elaine he had completed an enhancement, improvement program in prison.

Ron explained he had earned his high school diploma at Bridgeport Prison, and informed Elaine that the enhancement, improvement program had expanded his awareness and raised his consciousness.

"I learned about myself and about my world." Ron told her he intended to implement what he learned and improve his stature in society. Finally, Ron said, "I want to become somebody too."

Ron and Elaine learned about each other and appreciated the similarities but Elaine noticed they had arrived where they were by different circumstances. She told Ron she was proud of his determination to better himself and she commended Ron for no excuses, no blame of others and his accepted responsibility.

Ron was pleased and he saw no judgment of him by Elaine. She had accepted him and his circumstance; now he wondered how he might help Elaine with her goals.

Ron and Elaine entered into a relationship, one that was subject to many interruptions with their school commitments. They found time to visit a coffee shop or a diner on occasion, but a movie was a rarity. Each was highly motivated to finish school so little came in the way of that goal. They visited museums and sometimes went to a large mall but did not spend money on one another.

Elaine would earn her degree in Sociology next year. She became hyper and could not wait to graduate. It was her obsession and she constantly talked of it. Ron was very happy for her, but he had three years remaining before he would be graduating. Ron did not know the future for Elaine and him once she graduated. He would still be in college and Elaine would not. He seemed to brood over this fact and realized negative emotions would surface but he was able to subdue them with application of his antidote technique which had now become habit. He occasionally felt the pangs of fear when he thought of his relationship with Elaine. He short-circuited these with positive antidotes and remained positive with a thank you to Bridgeport.

Elaine's final year of college passed rapidly and Ron attended her graduation. He shared Elaine's joy over her accomplishment and delighted in her having attained her goal. Elaine sensed Ron's sincere support and compassion. She recognized great respect and appreciation for Ron. But was it love?

Following Elaine's graduation, the couple found it more difficult to spend time together but they remained in close touch. Ron had hoped Elaine and he could find more time for each other following her graduation. But he noticed her extra time had focused on her church and church activities. She certainly was applying her knowledge as a sociologist and enjoyed working with others in her church activities. She was a leader and organizer which took more time. However when they were together, Elaine was very aggressive in exploring his belief, church affiliations and commitment. Ron was uneasy about Elaine's constant reminders that he needed to belong to a church. He felt Elaine had his well being in mind but might be determining what the prospects were for their mutual future. She now became adamant about Ron joining a church and attending church regularly. She invited him to join her church and advised Ron to seek pre-church counseling in preparation for church membership. Ron told Elaine he was uncomfortable about her urgency but it seemed as though she didn't hear him and she ignored his remarks but she continued to push him.

Ron felt he would like to join a church and belong to a congregation, but he needed time to explore and search his church options. He had no immediate intention of joining a church. As each week passed, Elaine's church involvement increased. And, on occasion, Elaine and Ron were unable to get together because of her church commitments. In fact, Elaine had inferred that if he wanted to be with her, it would be in church or a church activity.

Elaine's friends and her pastor were becoming involved and encouraging Ron to commit to their church, but Ron was not ready to commit to any church and decided he would advise Elaine of his decision.

Their relationship soured over the church issue. Church was Elaine's entire life, and she wanted to make it Ron's life too. Ron was deeply affected because of his sincere feelings for Elaine. He soothed his sour feelings with greater commitment to work and studies. A promotion became his focus, and with advanced upper-level business courses at City College he filled the vacuum of Elaine's absence from his life.

A job promotion did occur. He was promoted to supervisor of department procedures, responsible for indoctrination of new employees. He took his promotion seriously and would help all new employees as he had been helped when he joined Cleveland Gear Co.

Good things can come in bunches. With Ron's job promotion came news he had made the Dean's List at City College. Ron could not wait to call Mr. Terrill about his good fortune. When Mr. Terrill was told, he said, "Congratulations Ron. More good things to come!"

Ron felt again the old void in his life. A feeling of desire and wants—or was it a true need? He sensed the need for a steady, loving relationship. Not a relationship involving satisfaction of his sexual desires, but a need of a long, permanent relationship. He was motivated to pursue his needs and place them on the front burner.

Work was satisfying and Ron was finalizing his second year at City College. School was going well. In less than two years, he would graduate. A college graduate! He could not believe it. Ron had related his, what he referred to, good fortune to luck. He read and remembered from Prison, this quote: "I don't believe in people who blame their circumstance for what they are or are not but rather I believe in people who know what circumstance they desire and if they cannot find it, will set out and create it." This was Ron's motto. He remained positive and worked to create his circumstance.

But the gnawing need kept resurfacing and Ron fueled his pursuit. He needed a relationship with a compassionate, lovely and friendly woman. He had been advised, by more than one fellow worker, to visit a singles club. "Check it out," they encouraged. He would do so.

The singles club he chose was the Spring Grove Club. He had received good comments and recommendations about the club. The Spring Grove Club was clean but it bothered Ron that the club served liquor. However, it was reported to be primarily a dancer's club. Ron was short on dancing and/or night clubbing experiences but he was confident since he was athletic. His first visit caused Ron to feel like a fish out of water. But he noticed several nice looking girls who were good dancers and managed courage enough to ask and dance with four girls. They all were friendly and agreeable.

On Ron's fourth visit to the Spring Grove Club, he met Helen, a brunette, with an attractive body. Helen and Ron hit it off from the very start. She loved to dance and she did not mind leading him through the dances. The evening ended and Helen and Ron agreed to meet at the Spring Grove on next Friday evening. Before parting for the evening, he learned she was a receptionist at an employment agency.

Ron met Helen on Friday evening at the Spring Grove Club. They enjoyed dancing together and Helen complimented Ron on his dancing. Helen was a gregarious, pleasant girl. They danced most of the dances together with Helen dancing with someone else on occasions, but Ron sat and watched her gracefulness in each dance.

In a short time, Helen and Ron were steady company. They went dancing an average of twice a week. The evenings Ron was not in night class at City College, Helen and Ron could be found at Spring Grove enjoying one another.

Ron could not imagine anyone liking dancing more

than Helen. He even suspected her of dancing up and down the hallways at her employment office. Helen began to encourage Ron to accompany her to other clubs in the city. He did so, but it became so time consuming and expensive that Ron became bewildered with the whirlwind relationship. Ron worried about his studies and his work. He really liked and enjoyed Helen's companionship but he could not permit work or studies to be affected. Helen returned affection to Ron and this enthralled Ron. Over and over Helen told Ron he was the best dancer. This was her primary requisite, Ron learned later.

Dancing and partying continued for two more months. Ron became convinced Helen was a party girl and that was her mission, to have fun and be the best dancer. He noticed that Helen did not refuse a drink and she asked him if he wanted to try some marijuana. This wore on Ron's conscious and he was especially uneasy about frequenting dance clubs where liquor was sold and drugs were readily available. He would not indulge in liquor or drugs. His memory prohibited it.

Ron tried, but without success, to visit with Helen and discuss each other's background, but Helen showed little interest in sharing their backgrounds. This suggested to Ron that although he might be a great party companion, she was not interested in a serious, permanent relationship. She had no further plans for the future other than partying and dancing.

Ron became tired and more confused with all the partying. He remained dedicated to his job and his studies. Ron decided Helen was great fun but not his type. He broke the news to Helen in a very gentle manner and said he would not be attending any more dance halls. Helen did not seem disappointed and they said goodbye and good night at the same time.

For several days after the declaration to Helen, Ron reviewed his life at the present and where he wanted to be in the future. Ron decided a permanent relationship was not in the offing. He had known Elaine and Helen, two distinct opposites and neither had come to fruition. His fault, he told himself; no further regrets. He was seeking another promotion at Cleveland Gear Co. and he would graduate from City College with honors. These were his short-term goals.

Ego/Mind Games

The residual from tragedy, confinement, and no relationship accumulates. Ron's job at Cleveland Gear Co. became routine and going nowhere. Two nights of classes each week over two years was testing Ron's patience. He could not wait for graduation—but wait he must.

Ron's thoughts focused constantly on his past. Ron's self identity was questioned: where he had been, what he had done, and the tragic life suffered were front and center in reflections. Reflections into his past had him traveling the avenue of negative thoughts and emotions. In all study and learning involved in the positive enlightenment program while in Bridgeport Prison, Ron had not learned about himself. Even though the therapist, Marvin, had spent time discussing the "little self" and the "Larger Self," Ron had failed to grasp an understanding of his true self. This was a serious vacuum in self-realization, a void existing in the present. Ron had not advanced in his spiritual awareness and understanding of consciousness. What he did know the "little self" accounted for the worldly self involved with the Ego/mind's games. And he associated Real Self, "Larger Self" to his heart and soul which were unfamiliar to him, something to do with his spiritualism. Ron's awareness and consciousness had not firmly associated with the universal Power Source which was his reality, "Larger Self." He had not advanced understanding to comprehend he had Spiritual Power and energy. A great positive Power that would eliminate his shame and guilt negative thoughts, emotions. Negative force always succumbs to positive Power supplied by the universal power, God's Source.

Ron had knowledge from his enlightenment studies at Bridgeport Prison about forgiveness. He appreciated the Power of forgiveness before and while in prison. Certainly, the great lesson in forgiveness, as told by the prison chaplain, of God's gift of his Son Jesus Christ to forgive us all our sins, had not registered. Could he not, or did he not, choose to believe his sins had been forgiven with the crucifixion of Christ and our redemption? Was Ron suffering of his past and self-persecution? Could he not accept God's Gift? And by not accepting God's Gift was he shackled by his errors, mistakes of the past? Even though he did not understand forgiveness, he was forgiveness's great beneficiary and certainly had experienced forgiveness's gifts. How could he not accept the gift of forgiveness unto himself forgiven by himself? The larger concept he had learned at Bridgeport—Redemption and external life in God's Heavenly Kingdom—escaped him. For his forgiveness, Ron was a grateful, gracious receiver. Furthermore, Ron was not aware, conscious of the gift of the Holy Spirit indwelling him since the redemption and baptism. He heard many times from his prison chaplain, "You are free of all your sins because of redemption and the indwelling presence of the Holy Spirit. He received instruction about the Holy Trinity: God, Son and Holy Spirit. Perhaps this was preaching and something he had accepted as an approbation. He had never spoken to the Holy Spirit to help him and guide him, so God's Counselor was ignored. Wisdom and knowledge Ron did not acquire but was his ghost of the future. Ron was involved once again with a vicious struggle with perception. He lacked in-depth knowledge and truth to fend off worldly perception. Lack of awareness and consciousness obliged him to project from within the world as he allowed his perception to see it. Ron's senses perceived the Ego/mind's world and that is his true world since he was unaware of any powerful Godly sense. His flighty mind was in a full gallop, here, there, and everywhere, with thousands of different thoughts each day. The mind and Ego were one and the same Ego/mind. Ron was not grounded in reality sufficient to resist the Ego/mind and his perception of the world was incorrect. It was a false perception, a false world. He was at war with perception and knowledge. He lacked the knowledge, awareness, and consciousness to compete with perception. His knowledge was shallow even though knowledge is truth, truth is knowledge and perception is false.

Ron functioned the three years after parole with momentum acquired in prison. The freedom he experienced was the main energy source behind his momentum. Cleveland Gear Co. and a good job advanced him into financial security, and City College attendance contributed to his intellectual security. But it appeared Ron was no longer feeling the vicissitude of his freedom. He lost his freedom again. The Ego/mind phantom made enormous desires and wants, demands. The great desire and wants served as shackles securely imprisoning his mind, heart, and soul. He was prey for the tightening grasp of the insane Ego/mind curse.

All of his desires for more money necessary to acquire the world's material goods resurfaced with greater intensity. Formerly Ron had been satisfied with his earnings which provided for all immediate needs. But suddenly the resurfacing of a thirst for material possessions had consumed his financial resources. It had little to do with needs but rather with imaginary, illusionary desires and wants. He was on a desire/wants spree attempting to satisfy old friends, the Ego/mind and the little self.

Ron now made a major purchase. A possession he needed and deserved. He purchased a three-bedroom home in a middle class suburb. Ron had the down payment and the lender amortized the principal balance on a thirty year, 5% interest rate annualized at $485.00 a month payment. The installment home payment was his only payment on debt. Ron followed the home purchase with aggressive purchases of furniture and appliances for the new home. He exhausted his remaining cash. But he had not quenched his thirst for more desires and wants and this did not stop him from spending on more possessions. He had learned, and it was readily available, the monthly installment payment-as-you-go pay system. He committed to debt and the installment purchase plan as he played the Ego/mind game.

As Ron's monthly installment buying began, he learned of the credit card scenario. Ron succumbed immediately and applied for three credit cards simultaneously. The individual credit and plague struck too. It struck suddenly and he enjoyed walking into a store flashing his newly acquired resources and walking out as the possessor of still another desire and want. Time after time it happened. Accounting for his cash-in flow and cash-out flow balances never existed until suddenly credit cards were no longer accepted in the stores. He had "maxed out." Ron realized that resources were gone; no installment credit, no credit cards, and no cash left over from work checks.

The Ego/mind paid him no slack and the desires and wants continued. He projected out through senses and perceived many desires and wants. He always was able to convince himself, "I need this, I deserve this" and "I can find a way to pay for it." He believed everything the Ego/mind envisioned for him. But as he moved in his new neighborhood, he observed shiny new cars, big boats, motorcycles, and all sorts of toys. He felt he needed them. He bought them on credit as credit permitted.

Because someone said in Ron's presence that he had six credit cards, Ron felt shorted. *I can use more plastic too.* He applied for three additional cards and received them. The new buying power had his twisted, separated mind racing to determine his next purchase. He continued to buy and his home had possessions within and without suggesting wealth. He must be wealthy. The Ego/mind's new follower was praised for false perception and directly caused more debt and closer to financial failure.

Ron was in big trouble. Ron's good job could not generate cash to meet monthly payments. He was feeling the stress and very uncomfortable. What to do? He began the popular credit card game. He used the credit card balance from one card to pay another credit card payment due—and some others overdue.

Ron was suffering from a disabling illness, no doubt. It would have been better for Ron if he suffered a disease—but not the Ego/mind illness, ultra egoism. Science can treat a disease with an antibiotic, and cure the disease. Penicillin, a great scientific discovery, has saved many lives. Blood poison was treated with penicillin and then suddenly disappeared. However, penicillin could do nothing for his poisonous illness, egoism. Ron suffered on and on with egoism—the solution for eliminating egoism was not more credit. Credit was gasoline on fire. Ron had to live with self-created suffering or find a solution. Where might Ron's illness take him? Many times melancholia or depression result, and even insanity. But more prevalent issues occur, e.g., crime and murder. His illness untreated, Ron was swirling down, down a spiral into a deep abyss from which he might never return. The Ego/mind had killed again.

Ron needed to understand the evil, treacherous, and debilitating nature of false perception the working partner of the Ego. He needed to understand it is the devil, it is illusionary and unreal. Ron needed to escape the separation of his mind and the "Larger Self." He must see universal awareness for goodness through Power's Source, God's power. Ron must see through awareness and consciousness, universal energy source of power from empowering thoughts and feelings of love, joy, peace, kindness, etc. available to his "Larger Self" and he can draw the energy from the abundance made available by our Source, God. If Ron could do this, and he can, he would avoid being another Ego/mind casualty.

Ron faces another crisis as he solves his dilemma through universal energy Source, God, because the Ego/mind has nothing to do with positive thoughts and feelings, or God. The Ego/mind will resist, and Ron must be ready for battle. Ron must begin by changing his allegiance and feature a new identity. He must begin by inner projections made positive so he sees the world of peace, love, kindness, truth, friendship, and contentment. This perception is positive and truthful and negates the false perception of worldly prized goods and possessions. The positive thoughts and feelings involving powerful energy will replace negative thoughts and weak energy that is disempowering.

Ron would need to recover from his illness through empowering thoughts and feelings. He would need to discern and discover his basic needs versus desires and wants. He will make peace with himself when he discovers that his basic needs are food, clothing, transportation and not much else—and his worldly gifts and possessions he can do without. The energy from self-peace is sufficient to power him onward.

Ron needed to refinance credit card debt and installment purchase debt. Refinance effort is extended to borrowers with truth and commitment for strong effort. Through understanding and love, creditors readjust monthly payments. Ron was energized by the power, truth, honesty, love, and friendship in dealing with creditors. The initial awareness and consciousness of the power of individual energy, Source comes from within, Ron's "Larger Self."

Ron created still another setback. He had lost a positive attitude for work. He displayed little joy and contentment toward fellow workers and work. He was not as assured and in control of himself. Supervisors at Cleveland Gear Co. had bypassed Ron for a second promotion he deeply desired. He continued on a course of more gloom and frustration. The fatal blow dealt himself was that he dropped out of City College. He had three quarters left at school to be granted his degree, a B. A. in Business Finance. Ron was spinning downward and backward.

Ron still had his job and he gathered himself and re-dedicated energy and ability hoping to earn the next available promotion.

Ron was feeling ill at work these days, especially in the morning before he could get in gear. The feeling carried over into his work on some days. He felt lightheaded and was subject to a floating sensation. He began to forget and was absent-minded with longer periods of daydreaming. It affected work and he realized it. Ron persuaded himself to fight these symptoms and rallied thoughts and energy toward work but it was very strenuous and he came home without energy. Ron had lost some interest in life and his home had suffered need of up-keep. Ron drifted into long periods of daydreaming and he suffered from melancholia. His melancholy caused him to blindly stare and his mind was blank. He continued to deteriorate and lost several days of work. Some days he could not or did not get out of bed. He felt dreadful and told himself he could neither cope with work nor cope with others.

One day while at work, Ron was summoned to the main office. He was told he must see the company doctor. Ron was placed on sick leave. A shock for Ron since he had no idea the company officials had observed his plight. He hoped the doctor could help him get well. He was feeling sorry for himself because he knew he had let himself, Mr. Terrill, and Judge Lowell down. Ron was suffering a sorrowful negative mood.

Ron's illness progressed and he fell into depression. Melancholia left him sad, and depression caused him to be fearful. He suffered fears mostly imagined. He was full of gloom and sadness during depression. Ron's company doctor would address his depression.

The first step in depression treatment was a complete physical. Biologically Ron's body was sound but, after review of psychological tests, there was indication of extreme inconsistencies and thought/mind activity. The company doctor referred Ron to a psychological specialist and a psychiatrist. The specialist, upon testing and evaluating, diagnosed that Ron was suffering from depression but not major depression (clinical depression). The doctors explained to Ron, "Your depression is not entire body illness that affects your physiology. Your body remains strong and we want it to remain strong so we need to treat your dysthymia, a form of depression.

Ron asked, "What is dysthymia?"

The doctor responded, "It is not major depression, it is far less severe but untreated can become progressive depression." Ron felt better with the doctor's remarks.

The doctor further explained, "You suffer from long-term chronic symptoms that do not completely disable you, but keep you from feeling good or from functioning full throttle. Mr. Wilson, perhaps I can compare it with chronic infection, you never develop a full-blown disease but you always feel run down."

Ron nodded his head in agreement and uttered, "Sounds like me."

The doctor proceeded to explain the causes for dysthymia. "You may have been born with a tendency to experience a depressive mood. It may also be caused by childhood trauma, adolescence problems, difficult life experiences, trauma from losses, unsolved life problems, and chronic stress."

"My gosh," blurted Ron. "This is the story of my life."

The doctor told Ron that about 5% of the population suffer from dysthymia. Most persons respond favorably from psychotherapy and using a drug, e.g., Xanax or Prozac and others prescribed.

"Finally, Ron, we are concerned about a situational depression that we will treat, it is very treatable."

Again Ron asked, "What is situational depression?"

The doctor answered, "Situational depression is usually shorter term than dysthymia; it need not be. Situational depression is the result of an identifiable stressful life situation as a death, a divorce, loss of job, financial difficulties, an accident, abuse among many."

Ron nodded his head again and said, "Sounds familiar."

The doctor told Ron they must treat this illness to avoid deeper depression or a double depression episode. The doctor would advise the Cleveland Gear Co. doctor of the diagnosis and the recommended therapy. The psychologist asked Ron about his sickness and vacation time benefits. Ron advised the doctor he had one week's vacation time coming and he had accumulated four weeks of sick leave time. The doctor decided to recommend a four-week therapy treatment to the company. "After four weeks of psychotherapy, Ron should be ready to resume work. We can regulate the drug treatment while at work and will make appointments for continued psychotherapy around your work."

Ron expressed his desire to begin therapy immediately and he was hopeful he would feel better so he could resume full-time work.

What would his depression therapy entail? Ron hoped he would learn more about awareness and consciousness. Could therapists help him comprehend the real self ("Large Self") and how it serves well being through providing power feelings, e.g., kindness, peace, joy, love, etc. with high energy. He knew the real self, "Larger Self," had to do with positive feelings, love, joy, peace, kindness, and contentment. Perhaps the therapists could help him become familiar with true identify; he hoped so. He was tired of ugly feelings, uncertainty, fear, frustration, and anger. He must become a follower, a follower of his "Larger Self" and divorce the Ego/mind and "little self."

In therapy, metaphors and allegories are often employed. These can help patients understand their situation better. A metaphor or allegory can awaken patients to reality and start them on the road to greater awareness and higher consciousness. Ron recalled a great lesson in reality and awareness he learned at Bridgeport Prison. His therapist there told him about Saint Anthony in the desert. When Saint Anthony was asked how he would differentiate between angels who came to him humble and devils who come in rich disguise, Saint Anthony responded, "You could tell by how you felt after they departed. When an angel left you, you felt strengthened by his presence. When a devil left you, you felt horror." Depression is a devil and leaves you in horror.

As Saint Anthony was alone in the desert, Ron had been alone in his own desert and had been visited by many more devils than angels. Ron had felt the disempowering energy of horror more than once in his young lifetime. It is time for angels to visit Ron. Can therapists teach Ron the manner necessary to invite angelic presence unto himself? Ron felt therapy would be his bridge that permits passage over the Ego/mind's world into the world of real self, "Larger Self" which employs great, positive awareness, and high consciousness. He was ready to utilize universal energy, power from his Source, God.

Back at Work

Two months passed since Ron's therapy. He was back at work at Cleveland Gear Co. and they were happy to have him. He was one of their young financial minds in the company.

Ron Wilson's attitude had improved during his therapy and demeanor suggested he had regained control of emotions and feelings. Ron was relaxed and appeared content. He was doing more and better work without his customary emotional disturbances. His attitude toward fellow employees was more open and friendlier. Ron was relaxed and comfortable around fellow workers. Fellow workers were pleased. They liked Ron.

Ron's job at Cleveland Gear Co. was secure and he was granted tenure. His company included Ron in their long-term plans.

In small measure, Ron's financial situation improved. He was able to bring his home mortgage current. Ron was able to keep in abeyance credit card harassment for delinquent payments. He made the payments he could and negotiated some payment relief with lower payments. Payment balances were gradually reduced. Ron had negotiated monthly installment payments from "binge" buying purchases so he was current. The payments frustrated him because they involved purchases he did not care about any longer. It was hard having to spend cash on things he no longer cared about. Ron had become no financial "whiz" but it was of necessity he took hold of his financial responsibility.

During Ron's recent therapy, it was revealed to him that much of his stress and frustration stemmed from foolish spending. He was told to stop spending and pay attention to basic needs. He had been advised how to confront overwhelming debt with truth and honesty. He must admit his financial problem as his own and then take responsibility. Honesty with himself was the beginning of his ability to disclose his financial situation to his creditors. Honesty with himself provided honesty toward creditors. He observed, *the more honest I am to myself the more honesty I have to offer.* This awareness made him feel good about himself. He regained a measure of pride with each financial responsibility he accepted and pride increased as he negotiated each debt.

Ron enjoyed his recent therapy. He had many one-on-one interviews and discussions with his therapist. Each day the patients had group panels and discussions. He enjoyed the group sessions. In the group exchanges the sharing seemed helpful. He learned greatly from others who were sharing their experiences. Sharing was very therapeutic. From group discussions, Ron observed and began to comprehend that other persons were suffering from similar negative feelings as he suffered. It was informative and also comforting to say he belonged to a group. He discovered that his depressive, negative feelings and moods were identical with others, even though causation might not be the same. He concluded following group therapy, negative emotions and feelings were not solely his.

His individual discussions centered around family and family relationships. He was told to release the burden of shame he possessed due to his dysfunctional home. Therapists professed that shame was due to guilt feelings he harbored. He must not hold himself guilty for his home environment. Because of shame feelings due to self-guilt persecution, he experienced moments of unbelievable fear. Fear caused him to mistrust himself and others and his irrational fear served as a shield prohibiting trust of himself and others. Ron was told the reality of all negative feelings was inability to see shame, guilt, and fear as unreal, illusionary. They do not exist anymore than other negative emotions, feelings, exist. They were the results of your false projections and your false perception. Your false perception of the world engineered by the evil Ego/mind and little self-partnership is a present to you, gift wrapped full of negative emotion, feelings and utter chaos for everyone who accepts the gift, egoism.

"Ron," the therapist told him, "you are suffering from very negative emotion, feeling as by-product of your egoism. You demonstrate hate, anger, and envy; all disempowering, negative emotions and feelings as much as you do shame, guilt, and fear. They are bed partners dreaming in the unreal, illusionary world of your Ego/mind."

Therapy was very structured and organized with detail. The patients got out of bed at the same time each morning, ate their meals on a regular schedule, had their discussions; their group meetings at regular times, and went to bed at a set hour. The structure of the therapy was to subject the patients to organization and detail. The patients lacked these skills in their personal life.

Ron had been sheltering blame for a lifetime. He blamed himself for many of his family problems. He would also blame family for much of his personal problems but he was told to release parents of the blame and take hold of his life, that only he is accountable for it.

Ron was told to stop living in the past. "There is no past as well as no future time, release it, it never existed, it is gone forever. What is the old adage, you should not cry over spilled milk."

Ron was told to focus on the only realistic true time, Present Time.

"Ron, take care of the present time, forget the past and it is useless to fret about the future. The reason is obvious, Ron, think about this. Why waste present time on the spent past or the nonexistent future? Ron, you live in the present time, Holy instant, second and no more or no less."

Ron admitted to himself he had difficulty understanding, comprehending what was said in his discussion but he did realize he had better feelings and positive feelings, especially about fellow workers and about himself. He felt gracious toward Cleveland Gear Co., his employer. Ron felt some peace; he was calm, even joyful at times and more content. His awareness was obvious and a greater level of consciousness prevailed. Therapy helped Ron substitute positive emotion for negative emotion. Ron reverted to "antidote" therapy learned at Bridgeport. He was substituting positive emotions and feelings in place of negative emotions and feelings.

Ron's period of "bliss" continued for three to four months and then old pangs of desires and wants accompanied by old familiar negative emotions and feelings "dumped" on him. He struggled with this problem for a time, and a new approach to combating it worked for a time but eventually he gave up. He was not able to submerge these negative thoughts and feelings, or he was not willing to, and unwilling to drown them. They continued to progress and cause pain and grief. Ron was "backsliding" with negative ways. He told himself he was sincerely making an effort to overcome this resurgent temptation.

But he seemed unwilling to ask his will to make a correct choice and rid himself of this "stinking thinking."

Ron joined his Ego/mind little self and went on an illusionary Ego/mind spending spree which momentarily subdued ugly feelings and he was at peace, for now, with the Ego/mind little self-relationship. Any reprieve from the Ego/mind demands was short lived and the Ego soon resumed its demands. The Ego was displeased and needed greater satisfaction, more gifts. What could he do? He had again spent cash he saved and at the same time had "maxed out" credit cards again. The desires and wants grew stronger as the Ego/mind pressed him for more of the world's goods. What did the Ego know of Ron's finances and, further, it made no difference to the Ego.

Ron panicked. He overextended his credit cards. Credit card companies demanded payment, which he was unable to meet; demands were insistent and their insistence became harassment. Finally, Ron missed a home mortgage payment. Ron was "backsliding" day by day as if on a journey headed for disaster. He was in a frame of mind to do whatever to satisfy the Ego/mind demands. Ron was in great debt, deep trouble. He needed a quick fix, a salve-like relief from the burning financial sore he had created. He visited the bank that held his home mortgage. The bank loaned Ron $5,000 with his home as collateral. The bank had a first and second mortgage on the home. Ron had very little equity remaining in his home. The disaster warning bell had begun to ring and its sound was deafening.

Ron's perception of the world had not changed. His false perception had not varied and the Ego/mind ingenuity taught him advanced financial skills necessary to keep in stride with illusionary desires and demands. Ron developed a gluttonous appetite and was indulging in every worthless worldly possession available to man. His acts were veiled by indignation. *It's unfair how I am treated!* The ugly, negative thoughts and feelings began to overwhelm him and he detested being at home alone. He continued to "backslide" and was becoming desperate searching for help. He had hit bottom, he had willingly lost his identity and respect to his enemy the Ego/mind little self. But what help?

In the interim, Ron created for himself an illusionary shopping phenomenon called "window shopping." These people crave, live by the fear of scarcity, and are without resources and must always buy, even if it is imaginary. Ron continued to buy without resources and he continued to own if for only the time he gazed in great desire and want. This moment it was his. This was fantasy but it resulted in response to a question, what to do? Also, "window shopping" seemed to quiet the Ego/mind's demands for a time since the fantasy of owning must have matched the fantasy the Ego/mind were living in an illusionary world. As soon as Ron ceased "window shopping" and daily trips to the mall, the chimes began chiming and the Ego/mind's crescendo, "We desire and want more" began. So off to the mall and more "window shopping."

Ron Meets a Stranger

This Saturday Ron was on a regular "window-shopping" spree. He cherished the satisfaction of owning even though it provided ownership, an illusion, in his mind. It was a very peculiar ownership satisfaction. His shopping had no ends. He could buy whatever he wanted. He need not pay attention to cost, it didn't matter. He could buy anything and own it for the amount of time he stood before it and marveled at its presence. How powerful and wonderful Ron felt with all this window buying-ownership. It is simply insanity. Ron always lavished praise and satisfaction upon each purchase as a true owner; however, now he had to leave it behind. What a loss without real ownership, he sensed. Ron made many temporary purchases and had many temporary ownerships. Ron prepared to depart the Mall of America. He felt a feeling of uselessness draining him and he knew he was in a helpless state.

As Ron was walking past a resting bench, he was looking for a place to rest and people watch. Sitting in a quiet, unoccupied area, a person spoke to him, "Are you experiencing an enjoyable day? Are you finding what you need? Can I help in any way?"

Ron was startled; he viewed a pleasant, clean dressed man in white shirt and white pants and with beautiful white groomed hair. He seemed so clean, peaceful, kind, content and very pleasant.

Ron was tongue-tied; he did not know how to respond. Finally he said, "I am tired, thank you, but I have seen nothing I need." The stranger disappeared apparently involved with someone else.

The brief encounter found Ron surprisingly calm, peaceful, and not deeply disappointed with his "window shopping" results. He considered this strange, as a normal "window-shopping spree" left him moody and unfulfilled. He left the Mall for the parking lot and found his car and went home.

Ron's fantasy world continued at home. He had purchased several video games and video movies. His game and movies were all fantasies and not corrective in nature. Ron spent many hours each evening at home fantasizing over worldly desires. In his wildest dreams he had many possessions. Ron had little contact with the present and the present second was spent in the unreal world. Ron liked fantasy world since he did not know the real world and could not live in the present time.

It was Saturday. Again Ron went to the Mall of America. He was "window shopping." He had no cash. Ron left home early to avoid harassment by creditors.

Ron circled the Mall and came to the rest area. He again spotted the same neatly attired man, all in white and gazing around the Mall. Ron purposely moved toward the man and said, "Hi, and a good day to you! You must frequent the Mall regularly."

The man answered, "Only as much or often as I need." Ron wondered about the need he was speaking of, but Ron knew it not polite to pry into personal matters with a stranger so he dropped the matter.

The stranger calmly, happily, and politely spoke to Ron. "It appears you are unable to find what you are searching for, may I be of assistance?"

Ron recalled the stranger had asked a similar question last Saturday and wondered how he should respond.

He said, "I have been searching for something for some time but I have looked, searched, and have not found it."

In response the stranger said, "Sometimes a person needs special attention and assistance before he knows what it is he needs. Perhaps you lack the knowledge, truth to know, and your perception is not helping you."

Ron was perplexed and questioned the reality of the stranger. He seemed so likeable and kind, and sincerely desiring to help Ron. For an instant Ron was considering disclosing his enormous thirst for desires and wants to the stranger. However, a person on the opposite side of the rest area drew Ron's attention. He had demonstratively indicated to Ron he would like to meet him. The man was attired in all black, with slicked back, coal black hair. His black, pencil mustache was pronounced and unforgettable. Ron excused himself from the man in white and walked toward the man dressed in all black.

Upon reaching the slick looking person, the slicker extended his hand and said, "Hello, you have come just in time." Ron replied, "Hello to you and why do you say I have arrived just in time?"

The stranger in black with the astonishing penetrating dark eyes and matching black pencil thin mustache said, "I am looking for an associate who can assist me in my very successful, entertaining, and ever-growing enterprise."

Ron's mind was racing and very inquisitive as to what this enterprise could be and how it would benefit him, a stranger. He asked, "Just what enterprise, business are you speaking of, and how might I fit in?"

The stranger quickly replied, "We are the most prosperous, successful enterprise in the world. We live in the real world and we continue to grow, expand, and we offer rewarding opportunities for everyone. If you want money, worldly goods, whatever possessions you desire, and tremendous sensational experiences, we are your savior." Wow!

Ron felt a deep tug at his heart and the heat from his racing mind hardly made it possible for him to respond. But he did not hesitate, he had been aroused. Ron wanted to know what he could do to become a part of such a worldly enterprise. He asked, "What will I do in your business?"

The stranger slowed down and said, "I don't even know your name." He was baiting Ron. "What is your name?"

Ron responded, "I am Ron Wilson."

"Well then, Ron," said the stranger. "We control the entertainment business throughout the country and parts of the world. We are in a sure thing business and loaded with cash, a no failure business. We deal in casinos, liquor, sports, and politics."

Ron was startled. How would he be of any assistance since he had no experience in any of these enterprises? Ron was puzzled and much less enthused now, but asked, "Can I work with you on a part-time basis because I am reluctant to leave my accounting job?"

"Ron," the stranger answered, "we are mostly part-timers and you most assuredly can continue your present job. Ron, I am returning here next Saturday and I will have a proposal for you. Are you interested?" Ron replied, "Yes, I will be here next Saturday."

Ron had been surprised by two distinct, different persons, one a very kind, calm, pleasant, assured fully contented person who made him feel restful and at peace. The other stranger was boisterous, very certain, very arrogant, egotistical with a mind tempered by worldly riches. Ron had a feeling of uncertainty, suspicion, and restlessness in his presence. However, he had made an appointment with the nattily dressed stranger and he intended to keep it.

Saturday came and he went again to the Mall of America. He ventured directly to the rest area and confronted the man dressed in white. He was calm, reassuring, and peaceful as always. In the stranger's presence, Ron again became immediately alert and was eager to ask questions of the stranger. To Ron he was no stranger; he seemed to be a long time acquaintance Ron had lost touch with unfortunately.

Ron asked, "Are you retired or still working? What is your job?" Ron felt he could be personal now and hoped the stranger did not mind. The gentleman replied, "I have been employed for a lifetime, an eternity, I am not retired and my work is very rewarding. My work entails teaching and counseling with a universal very powerful Source. We assist persons to find themselves and we direct them on a very special path. I take great pleasure in teaching the truth, knowledge, and understanding to unfortunate, uninformed souls."

Ron responded asking, "Where do you work, where do you live, what are the financial rewards?" The stranger said, "I work everywhere, whenever needed, I live in the universe, my rewards are infinite, enormous, I cannot count them."

Ron's curiosity overwhelmed him, he wondered if he could work with this man, but he could not resist any longer. "Can I work in your endeavor, what will be granted me for security so I need not worry about my existence?"

The stranger replied, "Yes, by all means, there is room for you in my work and the work's primary benefit guarantees that all your needs are fulfilled and you will never yearn for another worldly toy. Whom I represent guarantees: external life, joy, happiness, love, kindness, contentment and everlasting peace. Ron, you are witnessing and feeling some of the treasures and rewards this very moment. Each moment of your existence will be the same, always. You will not be concerned with the past or the future."

Ron did not know what to say, but he appropriately asked, "How do I sign on for this position? I want to become a part of such an endeavor."

The response, "I will explain later this afternoon after you complete your other interview. I will meet you here precisely at 5:00 P.M. It is now 2:00 P.M." He left.

Ron wondered, *How did he know that I had another interview? I never mentioned to anyone my afternoon's meeting.* Ron felt the electricity and energy from the visit with the man in white. Ron never expected he would need all the electricity and increased energy for his next interview.

The stranger in black got right to the task. He sensed he might be losing the battle for Ron. And the slicker wondered if he was losing his touch. He would dangle all his worldly riches at Ron and assure Ron that they would be there forever and never in limited supply. He would make an offer which Ron could not refuse.

Ron greeted the stranger, "Hello, how are you today?" To Ron it appeared the stranger was weary, uncertain about himself but very urgent to get on with the offer.

The stranger spoke, "We offer you all the money you will ever need, all the cars, all the best clothes, and worldly pleasures known to man. You only need to ask and we will provide you with every worldly want and desire. It is an offer you cannot assign a dollar amount to but one that will make you a millionaire over and over. That is what you desire, Ron, to be a millionaire, isn't it?"

Ron could not believe what he heard. He was short of patience realizing this is untrue, a gimmick . . . how can it be true? His emotions had come 360° in 15 minutes. He was drained of energy, he felt suddenly ill, and he could not understand such swings in feelings. Was his Ego/mind little self rushing him into something from which he could never return? His very existence was being challenged and why, how come?

The stranger had made Ron his offer and was in great hurry to have Ron follow him. "I will take you to visit many of our worldly enterprises, I will allow you to experience as much or all of our worldly pleasures that we are engaged in. Come let us be on our way?"

Ron paused, he was being overwhelmed and he was in a state of bewilderment. He reminded himself in an hour's time he was to meet with his other stranger friend. Ron finally said, "I cannot accept your offer or your invitation since I have another commitment. I will give you an answer next Saturday." This was a very hurtful set back for the stranger and he said, "I will need an answer by 6:00 P.M. tonight. Here is a number you can contact me." Ron took the card.

The closer 5:00 P.M. came, the more Ron felt calmness, peacefulness, and contentment. At 5:00 P.M. he appeared at the rest area and was very excited to learn of the benefits from his new friend. They greeted each other and Ron was pleased he did not have to ask about remuneration if he joined the friend's enterprise. The ever calm, joyful, and pleasant friend said, "You will be rid of your worldly desires and wants by releasing your Ego/mind, you will be guaranteed your little worldly self disappears with the Ego/mind. Your awareness will grow in leaps and bounds as you identify the fleshy world and all its false perceptions. Also, with increased awareness, you will acquire a higher level of universal consciousness so you may identify with your real self, your Larger Self.

"As you learn about yourself, you will grow spiritually and recognize true power, energy and Universal Source. I will be your teacher, counselor and direct you on your path to eternal life. You will never die, only your body will die and your Soul will live forever, your Larger Self. You have been guaranteed eternal life, I will help you realize it." It sounded great. Ron wanted to say, "Repeat this please," but he had sensed somewhere during the friend's remarks the Holy Spirit had helped him understand. Yes, the Holy Spirit which had been dormant within Ron. He was in a state of well being and embraced his gracious friend for the great gift of an unforgettable lesson and the gift of eternal life. Ron's decision was made, he would immediately release himself of his desires and wants. He would smother his little self. He would pay no attention to the world's representatives who offer all the fantasy of a split mind. He must call the dark suited, smooth talking evil tempter. He called and the devil was disappointed; however, he had many more to prey upon and he would begin immediately.

Truth and Knowledge Replace Perception

Ron had witnessed the duality in the world, Evil versus Good and he had confronted representatives of both Evil and Good. In his lifetime he searched for love, kindness, happiness, peace, joy, and contentment. He found it in a new friend, teacher and counselor. Positive emotions and feelings of peace, joy and love replaced negative feelings. Ron felt a sense of freedom. Worldly, sensual love had not been his but Ron was learning about true love and its power and energizing strength. His teacher would direct him in pursuit of the truth and knowledge of eternal love. Ron sought to emulate the new friend and acquire the new friend's positive qualities. *It is strange,* Ron thought, *I only know him as friend. What is his name?* It didn't matter, Ron told himself, I can address him as my friend, teacher, and counselor.

Ron was without a surname, address, or telephone number. How could he contact his teacher? His newly acquired friend told Ron he would be on a constant move and was going everywhere. *Where was everywhere?* Ron recalled a strange explanation the teacher made saying "You can contact me at any time day or night." He instructed Ron to go to his most quiet room and sit in silence. *Think of nothing, just be silent and I will come to you.* It was a surprise, Ron recalled, that he had been given permission to contact him any day or night. So why not now?

Ron entered the study-office of his home. It would be

quiet and it was equipped with a telephone, TV, and computer. His favorite recliner was in the office and he sat down in complete silence. He spoke directly to his friend, "It is I and may I visit with you?"

He paused, waited, and then asked interrogatory remarks, questions. "Do you hear me? Can I come meet you? Will you find me?" He had become rapid fire Ron again. One question right after another with no pause to allow for a response.

Several minutes elapsed and Ron's impatience replaced patience. He was disappointed that he had failed to contact his friend. He pleaded with him to respond. Finally, Ron said, "I will try again later."

That is all he said and he left the office. Ron went to the family room intending to watch TV but, before he could select a channel and settle in, a thought entered his consciousness. The thought reminded him he was to go to his quietest space and be patient, leaving all thoughts behind. He had not followed these instructions.

He left the living room and entered the bedroom. The bedroom was the quietest place in his home. He decided to sit on the floor resting his back against the side of the bed. He sat with arms crossed, folded in front of him and legs spread straight forward. He raised his head and stared straight ahead at the wall. Ron tried valiantly, and sincerely to stop all thoughts from entering his mind. He had a constant volley of thoughts entering his mind in a matter of seconds. He would close off a thought and another surfaced. He must contact his friend!

Again he asked, "Please, may I visit with you?" Ron sat still and remained silent, stopped thinking and waited and waited. His patience was restored while he waited and waited.

Then he heard a saying, "Have you been trying to contact me?"

Ron said, "Yes, about an hour ago."

"Oh, that was you?"

Ron questioned, "What do you mean, that was you?" The voice replied, "There was so much disturbance, noise, and garbled chatter, I could not tune in clearly. It was like a static disturbance, many voices talking at once and very fast, with no pause between remarks." Ron realized what had happened. He had lost his patience, he had shotgun-like thoughts filling his mind, in rapid order he was in a very disconcerting room.

The voice remarked, "You are here to learn more about the rewards for following me, in which award are you most interested?"

Ron responded without delay, "Love."

The voice replied, "I am grateful since all other awards are directly involved, the result of true love." Ron had not associated his feelings of peace, joy, kindness, and contentment as a result of love. This required more thought and reflection from Ron. Then the voice was heard again, "We will begin with a lesson in truth-knowledge versus perception and you will be taught about miracles that you will witness. You believe in miracles Ron, don't you? Contact me tomorrow, Ron."

Ron wanted to learn about miracles as much as love. He entered his bedroom and sat as before. Ron concentrated on clearing his mind of thoughts. When he was still, silent and his mind was not sending a volley of thoughts, he stared at the wall and asked, "May I learn from you today, please speak to me?"

He remained silent and waited patiently. He heard the voice; "We will concern our lesson with knowledge versus perception first."

Ron remained quiet and patiently awaited the voice to speak again. It did. "Perception and knowledge distinguish what is real and unreal. The world perception perceives is the world of time, beginnings, and endings. It is based on individual's interpretation and not facts, truth, or knowledge; perception is the flesh's world of birth and death. Perception is learned and selective in its perceptual emphasis, unstable, inaccurate in its interpretations. In perception we see a world reflecting our ideas, emotions, wants in our minds. It is projection from within you that makes perception. We look inside ourselves and decide the kind of world we want and then we project that outside perceptual world. We believe this is truth as we see it and often times it is false, unreal. We make it true by interpreting what it is we see. If we employ perception as justification of mistakes, our anger, our lack of love, we witness a world of evil, destruction, malice, envy, and despair. The result of many perceptual mistakes and what we see is not true. We distort our world by seeing what is not there, and perception is a function of our body; consequently, a limit on awareness. Perception sees through the body's eyes and hears through the body's ears. Our body is self-propelled by the intentions of the mind.

"The mind has a wonderful gift of will, free will by choice. Should the mind want to employ the body as an attacker, the body falls victim to richness, old age, and death. And, if the mind wills, chooses to accept the Holy Spirit's purpose, it becomes useful, positive to the end as long as it is needed. The body is neutral as is everything in the world of perception. The body may be used to satisfy the Ego's wishes or it can be used to please the Holy Spirit; this depends upon the mind's will, wants. The greatest misuse of the mind is the illusionary creation of the Ego. This is a separation of the mind from the usefulness of the Holy Spirit; and the mind partners with the Ego. The illusionary Ego preys upon your "little self" to the satisfaction of the mind which perceives mind and body as the sum total of earthly possessions: money, cars, titles, and endless worldly possessions. The more we own and gain, the greater our self image so we perceive. It is an illusion of the mind and untrue. Ron, we must learn to recognize these perceptual mistakes and must forgive ourselves. The distortions of our 'little self' concepts must be revealed in the truth of the 'Larger Self' for which we were created. The 'Larger Self' is the truth and who we are."

The voice paused, then asked Ron, "Can you see yourself without your credit card debt, without your frustration replaced with greater kindness, peace, joy, and satisfaction?"

The teacher did not wait for Ron's response for he knew the answer. So the voice continued, "Knowledge is truth under one law, The Love of God. God is Love and Love is God. The truth under the law cannot be changed. The law applies to everything God created and only that which God created is real. It has no opposite, no beginning, no end. It merely *is*. Knowledge and perception are opposite and two separate thought systems arise. With knowledge, no thoughts exist apart from God. The world of perception is structured in the belief of opposite and separate wills always in conflict with each other and with God. Here is perception's secret, Ron. What perception sees and hears seems real because it allows into awareness only what meets the wishes (will) of the perceiver. This creates a world of illusions, a world constantly in strife and conflict because it is not real."

The teacher paused again. "Ron, living in your illusionary world based on the law of 'scarcity,' we cannot acquire enough and your sense of self is one of inadequacy, incompletion, and weakness. The 'scarcity' law governs the whole world of illusions. And from the worldly point of view, we constantly seek, demand our desires and wants. We love another to gain something ourselves. This is what passes in the illusionary, dream world for love. This is a grave mistake because true love is incapable of asking for anything."

Ron was confused and needed some answers. Ron began by asking, "Since perception is false and portrays the world through body senses, e.g., eyes, ears, etc., then we cannot believe our senses, right or wrong?" The teacher answered, "Ron, you have cued into the false projection plague. Sensual perception is the result of your projection of what you want the world to be like and this choice, your perception, is submitted to your body senses. These senses make your projection as you wished, dreamed. The senses follow the desire. In reality you can believe and live according to your perceived sensual illusions, untruths."

The teacher paused, then resumed, "Do not be confused since the perception can also perceive the truth if this is what your will demands. You can demand your senses portray the world in the light of truth, reality. You do this by denying illusions, rejecting them, and setting aside your Ego/mind and 'little self.' This permits your 'Larger Self' as God created us to be what we are. Once the separateness of the mind is replaced through your awareness and greater consciousness of your Creator, Source, God, new tenants begin to take over. Your thought system and positive, high energy thoughts of love, peace, joy, and thanksgiving become manifest."

The voice continued, "The Holy Spirit, God's messenger, Counselor, and Teacher clearly and impressively speaks. If you desire to cease identifying with your body, the Holy Spirit comes to you with God's message of release, hope, and love."

The teacher asked Ron this question: "Ron, would you accept joyously the Holy Spirit's vision of Christ in exchange for the miserable picture of yourself? Christ's vision is the Holy Spirit's Gift. It is an alternative to the illusion of separation and sin, guilt, and death."

Ron asked, "How do I escape death?" The voice responded, "Repent of your sins and ask God's forgiveness, you will receive God's Redemption because God forgives your sins. Ron, you have God's pledge of eternal life in his Heavenly Kingdom and you will never die. Your Spirit, the 'Larger Self,' lives forever, eternally and your flesh, body and 'little self' die."

Ron now had an urgent appeal. "Where do I start? I want to accept love so that I can begin to share my love."

The voice stronger now answered, "I will open your third eye, the eye of imagination, so you can hear and see the true story. Since this is your starting gate, you must know the truth. God sent his son Jesus Christ to die on a cross at Calvary as atonement for all our sins. God's love for us was so great that he gave Jesus to us to forgive us of our sins. No greater love was ever given. God's great love and graciousness provided a gift of eternal life in Heaven. Ron, the best way to learn of love is to give love; then you receive more love in return. Love begets love. Your eye of imagination permits you to see God's love, witness God's love, and appreciate God's Gift. With your third eye, imagination, clearly see Jesus on the cross in Calvary and feel vast love displayed with open arms. Ron, you need to visit Christ at Calvary for the greatest gift of your lifetime; a message awaits you. We will discuss your preparation for a visit to the cross at Calvary and join with the greatest lover ever known, Christ."

The teacher stopped. Ron was afraid he would leave and he must ask a final question.

"Dear friend and teacher, what must I do in preparation for this trip? Can I ask you to show me the way?" The teacher answered, "Yes, I will help you and show you the way but first you need to prepare and I will assist you in your preparation. Contact me again, God's Speed."

Journey's Reward

The teacher observed Ron's unreadiness. He heard Ron's impatience. Ron was not ready for a final leg of his life-long journey. He would need further knowledge of the real world and the truth. The teacher-counselor would provide this opportunity to learn and obtain more knowledge and explain the truth. The teacher was grateful for the opportunity and cherished Ron's salvation. *I must patiently wait for Ron to call.*

Ron was distracted by the counselor because he had not explained what else needed to be achieved. Ron felt he was ready. He had committed to the new life. *Let me be on my way. What is the reward, at my journey's end?* He would not wait any longer. He must call his new friend, the teacher-counselor.

Ron entered the bedroom and took up his sitting position on the floor. He stared forward at the spot on the wall, then said, "Dear friend, may I prevail upon you?"

In the silence of his room, a voice responded, "I am ready to lead you on the last leg of your journey. Are you ready, Ron?"

"Yes," Ron responded.

The lesson began at the point of Ron's life where his illusionary vision of his world and the Ego/mind became his boss and tormentor. The voice said, "We are going to help you perceive the real world by reversing your perception mechanism. This reversal will produce positive, energizing thoughts and feelings such as love, peace, kindness, joy, satisfaction, and contentment—compared to the negative, disempowering feelings as shame, envy, jealousy, guilt, fear, and anger. You will be a different loving, peaceful Ron rather than a distrustful, frustrated, angry Ron. Here is how you manage this. Ron, are you following me?"

"Yes, I am."

"You must look inside yourself and see a different world, the real world you now seek full of love, peace, joy, kindness, and contentment. As you feel this, you project this world outside you and you immediately notice the difference from your old, unreal, illusionary world. You will first see the whole, entire universe and realize your new, real world is part of the entire universe. You will see beauty in all living beings—man, animals, and living nature sources, trees, water, sky, and land. This is your real world. Here you find the truth. The world and the vast universe you see is God's creation and you too are God's creation, you are part of this universe. It is yours to love, enjoy, use, and protect. The universe has your every need and you want for nothing. You feel love for this majestic universe which is your gift from your Power, Source, God. You have substituted through your Holy Will to choose the real world and you have rejected your illusionary false world and the Ego-devil.

"This is a miracle, Ron, one of many to come. The love you feel for all of God's creation has permitted you to see the real world, learn the truth."

Ron interjected, still clinging to his old world, "But how do I provide for all my needs and wants?"

The voice responded, "You must be persistent in your decision and believe that these provisions will go on as always. You must persist in your new belief and faith. When you remain persistent, you follow your goals, and never desert them. Even when you feel you are not succeeding or you have suffered a defeat, you persist and stay on course. But you look carefully at these transitory set backs and learn a lifetime lesson.

"Ron, God affords some setbacks in order for you to grow and learn. You make God's progress through life in His way.

"Another factor with persistence is temptation. When you are persistent and true to your goals, no temptations can result. Ron, your life to date has always lacked persistence and it has fallen to temptation again and again. Do you understand me?"

Ron said, "Partially, yes—but I am not clear about temptations and why do they occur?"

"Ron, this was the Ego/mind's desire for you to stay in misery and know a hell on earth. When you accept temptation, you see yourself to be miserable and tormented, otherwise you would never succumb to temptation. Temptation is the devil's strategy. Through temptation you become someone you are not. Know what you are and would be if not tempted and succumbing to temptation. Accepting temptation causes pain, madness, and death. Temptation leads to all of your past negative emotions and feelings; it ends positive dreams, squelches hope, and precipitates thoughts of death. You must know what temptation is and you must make a choice between temptation's journey ending in Hell or persistence's faithful, positive journey ending in Heaven. Temptation can convince you, you are your flesh, body, which must die.

"Ron, remember that God provided you with a precious gift of Holy Will, to choose without encumbrance, Hell or Heaven. Your confusion is due to a reverse sort of persistence shown you by the dying Ego and perpetrated by the evil-devil. You see God is permitting the Devil his last gasp and providing the devil an opportunity to hang himself. God's name works in reverse at times!

"Ron, God permits your concern about your needs, desires, and wants that the old world provided you so he could test your persistence to follow through and learn of the real world, God's universe and its abundance. You see the universe's abundance was intended by God to be available for everyone—not just you, but everyone. It is apparent for all to see that the universe's abundance never ceases whereas in your old world's lack of abundance, scarcity prevailed. Your basic needs will be provided by your present job. You will maintain your job and be richer in so many ways I cannot say—but you will be, since God rewards those who are believers, faithful, and persistent. But you need not worry since you are journeying away from scarcity. Abundance of energy, knowledge, wisdom and love is all yours.

"Ron, you need only to extend your love to whomever and whatever you encounter on your journey and an abundance of love will be yours; since the more love you give away, the more love you receive. There is one catch: Ron, you must *always be available and receptive.* Does all this make you humble?

"Humility is the acknowledgment of truth. You are seeking the truth and must be humble. Humility removes all your former pride, the false pride that led you into believing that what you own is who you are and very important. Your former pride leads to disobedience. You must be obedient, persistent, and loving on your journey.

"In our lesson today, a final word on forgiveness, as our journey's destination is all about forgiveness and love. Your new Real World is the result of complete forgiveness of the old world, the world you see without forgiveness. With forgiveness you see the real world and forgiveness removes all illusions which had distorted your perception and fixated it on the past. By forgiving you recall the loving thoughts you had in the past and those given to you. Ron, our eternal life is founded on forgiveness, the elixir of God's universe. When you forgive it makes you well. You receive kindness, love, everything good when you forgive. Inability to forgive leads to resentment, resentment leads to anger, anger leads to rage and who knows with rage?

"So, Ron, forgiveness will be your wave of momentum soaring you along on your journey. This wave of energy is far greater, powerful, and comforting than any you have traveled. Here is what you need recall. First, recall God's great gift of forgiveness when he gave His Son, Jesus, to die on the cross at Calvary for our sins. He forgives us!

"Ron, you must forgive yourself for your faulty perception and the creation of an evil world and you must forgive all your brothers, Sons of God, for their faulty perceptions. Forgiveness begins with God, through you and then to all God's Sons and creatures in the universe.

"How, you ask? You must forgive the weather you didn't like, forgive clouds you deemed ugly, forgive the birds that sang and you did not enjoy. You must totally, all inclusive, *forgive!* You must do this so all the universe and everyone, everything in it loves you and extend you love and powerful energy. Forgiveness is where it begins and where it ends. What questions do you have, Ron?"

Ron asked, "How can I remember all these life-restoring lessons?"

"Here is my plan for you. I will remain in your mind, heart, and soul verbatim and you will through synchronicity recall everything. Be persistent in your thoughts and know your helper will assist you when necessary."

The teacher asked, "Ron, are there any further questions?"

"Well, yes," Ron said. "How do I travel to my destination on this journey?"

The counselor said, "This will be revealed to you in your dream. For now accept that your travel agent is formulating your travel agenda. It will be planned directly from your repose state to your final destiny."

Ron was puzzled but had learned the teacher-counselor's advice had always been true. The voice dismissed itself and Ron saw that he had been in the presence of his counselor for two hours. He was exhausted and decided to forego dinner so he could go to bed.

In his deepest sleep he began to dream. In his dream all the wonderful, positive thoughts of the day began to lift his spirits. He was happy, full of joy, peaceful and excited. He was highly energized. Thoughts focused on his new world and especially with its abundance of unending opportunities. He felt himself in a state of kindness, bliss toward everything. He was generating so much universal energy that he felt ecstatic. The energy became so powerful it created an energy wave, an aura, and upon this aura Ron traveled toward his destiny, Calvary. It was such a peaceful, soft, flight that he was afraid he would ride on and on beyond Calvary.

Just then, he realized he was in the extended, loving arms of Jesus on the cross at Calvary. The cross, depicting the most powerful love known. Jesus' loving, tender embrace placed Ron's ear next to Jesus' mouth and he heard, "Amen, I say to you, today you will be with me in paradise."

Today Ron has never awakened from his dream and he will never choose to because he is in Paradise. In his new world, Ron lives in Paradise as promised.